PLEASE STAND BY

For Michele,
With Admiration

PLEASE STAND BY

A Novel

CAROLYN BENNETT

|N₁|O₂|N₁
CANADA

Library and Archives Canada Cataloguing in Publication

Title: Please stand by : a novel / Carolyn Bennett.

Names: Bennett, Carolyn, 1962– author.

Identifiers: Canadiana 2019015473X | ISBN 9781988098852 (softcover)

Classification: LCC PS8603.E55935 P54 2019 | DDC C813/.6—dc23

Printed and bound in Canada on 100% recycled paper.

Now Or Never Publishing
901, 163 Street
Surrey, British Columbia
Canada V4A 9T8

nonpublishing.com
Fighting Words.

We gratefully acknowledge the support of the Canada Council for the Arts
and the British Columbia Arts Council for our publishing program.

For Ian Gardner and Marion Robb-Gardner

COLD OPENING

The ER doctor packed her nose with sponges and left her inclined on a stretcher in the corridor, along with other patients who lined the wide thoroughfare. She studied the IV drip and speculated on the cool liquid entering her vein. Glucose and water, she guessed, or maybe an antipsychotic. That would be a graduation. *Now you can flip the tassel on your mortarboard. Hooray!*

Life would be different now.

No more lying on gurneys in crowded hospitals listening to the moans of the damned. No more being damned.

She glanced at the hospital ID band fastened around her wrist. Suzanne Foley. Her street address. Edmonton. She nodded. It's a start. An identity.

She stirred beneath a thin blanket. An ancient woman on another stretcher hacked primordial phlegm. Beside an elderly man slumped in a wheelchair sat Gordon, reading a magazine. He saw that her eyes were alert.

"Hey," he said.

She turned her head away and let a few tears escape. He stood over her.

"How're you doing? Suzanne?"

She forced herself to look at him. "All right."

"The bleeding has stopped. You may have to stay overnight."

"Did everyone see me leave in the ambulance?"

"Not everyone. Frank. Wilma. John. That's all."

She moaned. The ancient woman moaned.

"What happens now?" she asked.

"Well." He leaned in. "Do you really want to know or should I make something up?"

Her tongue and mouth were coated in a gummy film. She licked her lips to moisten them.

"Gord, thanks for being here. Now tell me."

"Have you ever heard the saying 'You're only as sick as your secrets'?"

"No."

"You will."

He tapped the side of the stretcher. "Rest up. I'll talk to the doctor and come back to pick you up."

Suzanne felt cool liquid in her arm and shoulder. A nurse whisked by in baby-blue hospital scrubs. She licked her lips again and asked the question she had wanted to for a long time.

"Are you single?"

"Am I single?" He smiled. "Are you hitting on me?"

"Maybe."

He looked into her eyes. "Why you drink so much? Why do you hurt yourself?"

"Why do you care?"

"Because you remind me of how I used to be. We'll talk."

She surrendered the word in a whisper. "Okay."

Wondering why he wanted to know, what it was to him and when they could talk, if he loved her without sickness, she crossed over into righteous oblivion.

She would be back, repaired and beaming.

PART I

CHAPTER 1—FADE IN: MEETING #1
EDMONTON, NOVEMBER, 2000

The Alberta Broadcasting System (ABS) was housed in a former rope factory on the edge of Edmonton. Edmonton dropped off past ABS, returning to field and gravel road. Legend had it that when the publicly funded broadcaster took over the space in an industrial park, a shipper discovered a noose dangling in a basement storage area. Throughout the years the story grew, long-term employees greeting new recruits with gruesome tales of hanging corpses. The newcomers who laughed usually went on to lengthy careers at ABS. Freelancers were a different breed. Employees kept the story from the freelancers, worried that the freelancers would visit the basement area where the noose was found, and calculate the distance from the ceiling pipe to the floor, factoring in their own height and weight and clunk.

Suzanne freelanced at ABS.

Swatting snow from her parka, she entered the building and trudged into an arid boardroom, fifteen minutes late for a meeting.

"Hello, Suzanne. We're doomed."

Leslie stood with his arms raised, his turtleneck damp under the armpits. Pauline and Gordon, the other freelance fundraising writers, sat at the conference table trying to busy themselves with their production schedules. Suzanne shuffled over to the refreshment table and poured herself a cup of coffee. She noticed a mild tremor in her hands. A tray of half-eaten donuts beside the coffee urn tempted her, but she resisted. That amount of sugar and fat could trigger an acid flashback.

"Hey, guys."

Gordon saluted and Pauline offered a wounded smile. The fundraising writers didn't socialize with each other outside the meetings. They all wrote at home and emailed their scripts to the producer. They only met three times a year to confab about the upcoming on-air campaign. Computer technology had made face-to-face conversation even more difficult for the solitary odd-balls. They would need each other now.

"These new guys are from Toronto, you know," Leslie said, fanning himself with his production schedule. "Aren't you from Toronto, Suzanne?"

"Good God, no."

"But it's where you came from."

"I only worked there. Briefly." Suzanne felt a rising paranoia. "Look, they can't sack us. They'd be insane to sack us."

"All I know is I have three cats."

"Yeah?"

"I have cats to support," Leslie said, selecting the remains of a Boston Cream.

Frank, the producer of the ABS on-air membership campaign, entered the meeting room, tapes and papers in tow. He had the gaunt energy of a marathon runner.

"Hi, guys."

Suzanne and the writers mumbled. Frank distributed sheets for them to ponder. He ran his fingers through his hair and rubbed his forehead.

"Okay. As you know, these are new times at ABS. Lawrence is no longer with us."

"You make it sound like he's dead," Gordon muttered.

"Well, that's not what I mean. There's been some change, and our on-air membership campaign is going to have a new look."

The writers groaned. Frank took a deep breath and proceeded.

"The new head of the network wants dynamism. Rather than have to wait for us to end our membership pitch, he wants viewers to tune in *for* us. He wants more show."

Suzanne glanced over at Leslie, who had raised his eyebrows.

"We are embarking on something that's never been done. Our mission is to make asking for financial contributions exciting."

"Exciting," Pauline said.

"Yes. That is the directive from John Brady. Make our pledge breaks entertaining."

Suzanne grimaced. Was this good news? Bad news? The four writers had been contracted by the Alberta Broadcasting System (the acronym ABS a definite misnomer) to write scripts for the station's on-air membership pledge campaigns. Every four months, the kindly and sincere ABS spokesman Lawrence Taylor asked viewers from High River, Great Slave Lake, Fort McMurray, Grande Prairie and other communities for financial support to help keep ABS a public television broadcaster. Lawrence, an avuncular presence in his early sixties, got behind the pitch, however repetitive and sonorous it was. Every night for three weeks, between such high-quality, predominantly British programs such as *Scientific Discovery*, *The Waggish Chef*, *Inspector Callaghan*, *Inspector Hawthorne* and *Who's Knocking?*, Lawrence appealed to the generosity of viewers, viewers who valued the high-quality, commercial-free programming that ABS broadcast. ABS had been Alberta's provincial broadcaster for decades because enough people donated money to keep the government from privatizing the service. The most "entertaining" the pledge breaks ever got was when Lawrence read a letter from an ABS member. This was the gig Suzanne desperately clung to, writing pledge breaks for an agency of the provincial government increasingly under attack for being moribund. Now they wanted a show? Who were *they*?

Frank checked his watch. "John Brady, and our new host, Jason MacLeod, should be here any minute."

Pauline folded her arms. Her papery lips were more taut than usual. "Frank. Are we expected to write entertaining things?"

"I would think so."

"How?"

"Well. You're all writers. You'll be able to come up with something."

"We haven't come up with anything new in three years," said Leslie.

"Yes, and I appreciate that, but I've been told that must change."

"I, for one, have no imagination," declared Pauline.

"Look," said Frank, "this is not my idea. I'm quite happy with the status quo. I had no problem with Lawrence at all. Apparently, focus groups thought he was too 'uptight.'"

"Focus groups?" Suzanne blurted.

"John has had focus groups in here, analyzing our pledge breaks. The general consensus was Lawrence is 'too stiff.'"

"Too stiff? How old were these people?"

"The eighteen to thirty-five demographic. They chewed up the set, the direction, the pace, the writing, the performance . . ."

Frank's voice trailed off. Suzanne doubted he put much credence in the jaded opinion of youth, especially youth that didn't watch public television. But a directive had come down from John Brady, the new guy in charge. Her face reddened.

"Frank, we're a provincial public broadcaster, the operative word in that sentence being 'provincial.' A gentle backwater. We don't need focus groups. Don't muck things up with analysis."

"Suzanne, please. Everyone, please. I understand you're frustrated and perhaps even upset. I understand how you feel."

"Do you?" asked Leslie. "Do you?"

Frank sighed. "Let's just hear what John has to say."

Suzanne pitied Frank, who had suddenly been thrust into the role of managing people after a permanent employee went on indefinite leave. Frank preferred cameras, lighting, stopwatches, the mechanics of television production. Dealing with the insecurities of writers visibly strained his patience.

There was a knock at the door. Marika, John Brady's glossy executive assistant, popped her head in.

"Frank, just want to let you know that John and Jason can't make the meeting."

"Oh. Okay." Frank paused and waited for an explanation. "Any reason why?" he finally asked.

Marika looked at Frank, shrugged her shoulders and left.

Frank turned to his confused team.

"Okay then. Well, we'll have to wait until next time for a meet-and-greet. For now, I'd say think about what has been discussed. Have you all received your script assignments?"

Four heads nodded slowly.

"Is everybody clear on what's happening?"

Four heads shook side to side.

Frank ignored them. "Okay. So I'll see you soon."

In the entire time Suzanne had worked at the Alberta Broadcasting System, Frank had never been the first to leave a meeting. Today he collected his papers, clipboard and tapes, kept his head low and ducked out ahead of the others.

We're fucked, thought Suzanne.

"We're fucked," said Leslie.

I'm fucked, she realized.

Chapter 2—Hey, Wilma

Suzanne let herself into the apartment and wriggled out of her parka and mitts. The phone rang. On the eighth ring Suzanne lunged at the receiver.

"What?!"

"Suzanne, it's Frank. The meeting is now tomorrow at eleven."

"Do I have to go?"

"You work here, so yes."

She slammed down the receiver. She had known about this shakeup at work for a while but overlooked its implications, opting to panic later. She flopped on her bed for an afternoon session of staring at the ceiling. The staring-at-the-ceiling session would probably be followed by a drinking-to-excess session. All this professionalism and meeting in person rattled her. She rubbed her face with rough, eczema-reddened hands.

How did she get to this place, this time in her life? Thirty-eight years old, unmarried, an anglophone Montrealer, attractive yet unadorned, chronic anxiety keeping her weight down and her eyes unnervingly wide, Suzanne had fled the flattening environs of Toronto and found employment in Edmonton. Alberta had outstretched its big beefy arms and held her in a friendly headlock.

Her apartment brought both enormous peace and stagnating angst. "Studio" was too industrious a word for her apartment. "Bachelor" didn't seem appropriate and "Bachelorette" sounded trivial. "Cell" suited the space. But it was her cell, a one-room sanctuary where she'd hibernated for three years. She had heard the various diagnoses from the medical profession—anxiety, depression, obsessive-compulsive disorder, borderline personality disorder, post-traumatic stress disorder, shingles—but the one that stuck came from a decrepit shrink posted in the subterranean murk of Toronto's Parkdale district.

"Have you heard the one about the woman, the chimpanzee and the shoehorn?" he once asked, smiling widely.

"Yes."

"Man, you know all my jokes. Every time I go to tell a joke you stop me and say you've heard it."

Suzanne had glanced at the psychiatrist's sole degree mounted on the wall: Bachelor of Arts, York University, 1965.

He leaned forward in his chair, paunch spilling over his belt.

"You know what I think is wrong with you? You? You have mixed feelings."

Even after all the years since the diagnosis, she still thought his assessment the wisest.

Suzanne liked Edmonton. Edmontonians said hello to each other in the parks. The first time someone said hello to Suzanne, she scowled. She had wanted to retain her eastern coolness, but eventually she submitted to Alberta's guilelessness. She even went to the Nashville North dance hall with Wilma, a fifty-two-year-old acquaintance from her building. She marvelled at the display of gender stereotypes: the macho cowboy and the little lady, twirling around the dance floor to the twang of new country, all boots and Stetsons and skirts and big hair. Suzanne bristled whenever she was called Ma'am. She bristled a lot at the Nashville North. On one excursion to the club, she shouldered her way onto the dance floor and slammed punk-style into a group of line dancers.

"What the hell are you doing?" shouted Wilma. "Are you hammered or what?"

The Nashville North line dancers continued their routine, ignoring Suzanne's flailing, until a black-clad, cowboy-hat-wearing woman shoved Suzanne into a table and punched her a few times. Wilma reluctantly stepped in and broke up the melee.

"All right, don't bother with this one. She's from Toronto or Montreal, one of those goddamn places. They don't know how to dance proper. Or how to be sociable," said Wilma to the black-clad, cowboy-hat-wearing woman. The woman, her fist ready to strike, held Suzanne by the waist.

"Okay," said Wilma. "you can have one more shot. Then enough."

Despite the beating and the sub-zero temperatures, or perhaps because of them, Suzanne felt at home in Edmonton. It reminded her of Montreal. Both cities had a low-level eccentricity.

Wilma. What was Wilma doing now? Suzanne rolled off the bed and went to investigate. She remembered the day Wilma moved in to the apartment building, two years ago. She was heading down to the basement with a pile of long-overdue laundry and had to pass some movers. Wilma's son, a doughy, pockmarked lad of around twenty, and three droopy friends struggled with an oversized brown couch. They plowed it into a wall and chipped off some plaster, even though the staircase was wide enough to accommodate it.

On the landing, Wilma barked, "For Christ's sake, Cody, stop being an ass!"

"Fuck off, Ma!"

Suzanne would later find out that Wilma had separated from her husband, a so-called "piece of shit." Suzanne commended her for having the bravery to leave a twenty-year marriage.

"The only reason I married the bastard was because he knocked me up!" Wilma informed her.

It took several months, but Suzanne and Wilma developed an acquaintance. Neither woman particularly liked the other, but settled for the distraction. They became a mutual, occasional habit.

Suzanne heard noise from the loud talk radio station emanating from Wilma's apartment as she approached the door down the hallway. She winced and knocked. Wilma answered, all five foot, three inches and one hundred and eighty-five pounds of her.

"Oh. You."

"Hey, Wilma. What's up?"

"Not much. You?"

"Work sucks. We're in limbo."

On the radio, a man complained about municipal taxes.

Wilma scoffed. "Yeah, yeah, so what else is new? You work and then you die. Well, come on in, come on in, no sense in standing in my doorway. You gotta smoke?"

"No, I thought you might have one."

Wilma's one-bedroom apartment had a thickness, a lethargic humidity that stupefied. The brown couch and accompanying chair invited lazing and weight gain. Wilma had covered the couch with crocheted quilts and leopard-print throw cushions. The apartment had green carpeting throughout, left by an ambitious former tenant. A small cabinet housed a collection of cat figurines, "from all over the world." A few bushy plants flourished by the living room window. On the large, square coffee table lay paperbacks and women's magazines. Wilma gave Suzanne the magazines when she finished with them. Suzanne enjoyed the predictability of *Women's World*.

"Do you want a drink? I have some rye."

"Yeah. Why not?"

A brochure that sat in Suzanne's top desk drawer flashed through her mind. *One of the hallmarks of alcoholism is the progressive loss of ability to drink according to intention.* What if her intention was to get annihilated? What then, brochure?

Wilma poured them two stiff tumblers. They clinked glasses.

"Happy days. Here's looking at you."

"*Mazel Tov.*"

"Muzzle what?"

"Never mind."

It was three-thirty in the afternoon.

CHAPTER 3—MEETING #1 REDUX

The next morning, Marika zipped into the ABS boardroom. "John and Jason are going to be late. But they will be here. Oh, and there's no muffins."

The overhead fluorescent lights buzzed.

Suzanne snapped. "We're dangling. Dangling. Just like the ghost in the basement. With the noose around his neck! I've heard the stories!"

"What stories?" asked Pauline.

"Nothing. Just relax," said Frank.

Pauline had a pinkish tint on her cheeks and purplish eyeshadow that accentuated her green eyes. The grey sweater and black slacks she wore made her look almost chic. Leafing through his binder and making notes, Leslie sat next to Frank. Gordon, ruddy with health and sipping bottled water, sat next to Suzanne.

"Where are the muffins? This is unacceptable," whined Leslie.

Suzanne cringed through a wall of pain. She pictured Leslie going berserk. *Man Restrained in Muffin Incident* the headline would read.

Pauline paused her intense knitting, put the needles down and leaned in. She lowered her voice.

"I hear there will be no more muffins. Ever. No muffins, no juice, no Danishes."

"Unbelievable!" said Leslie.

Never mind that the contract workers received no benefits like extended health care, life insurance, disability insurance or a pension plan. This deprivation was an affront to his dignity. No snacks?

Suzanne pressed her fingertips into her eyebrows. Her parched body and baked brain made her crack with intolerance.

"Leslie, what's the point in getting upset? If that's the case, that there's no muffins or cookies, so what? So fucking what?"

She swallowed a thin stream of vomit that bubbled up her esophagus. At least she had stopped heaving the thick porridge of last night's stomach contents. After spending the afternoon at Wilma's, drinking rye and forcing gaiety, the two acquaintances had stumbled into a cab and continued their interminable getting-to-know-you at a bar and grill on the concourse level of a downtown office building. Wilma had settled her bulk on a bar stool and flirted with the wizened bartender.

"Hey good lookin', what's cookin'?"

The bartender fixed on Wilma with burnt eyes. "You drink what?"

"Anything and everything!" she announced to the empty restaurant. Suzanne felt obliged to laugh.

They liked to play a game called "Around the World." They would imbibe, in order, the cocktails listed on the drinks menu, until one of them either picked up a man or vomited.

"Youz want a menu? Food?"

Suzanne grabbed some peanuts from a bowl and pointed at the first cocktail listed. "I have all the food I need. May I please have a piña colada?"

Suzanne drank all night, until her legs became noodles. Business concerns, meeting the new guys, all of it became secondary to the game. The game led to a gleaming track alive with electricity. The more she drank, the faster she sped down the track. She called it loco-motion. Nobody seemed to get it.

Now Suzanne crossed her arms so Leslie wouldn't see her tremulous hands. She glared at him, until her right eye twitched. She averted her glare to the poster on the wall behind him, a smiling family and the network's slogan "ABS: Come Home to High-Quality Television." In a larger, more sophisticated world he'd be a putz, but here in this burgeoning centre, he was a player.

"Hey, don't take your frustration out on me," he said. "There's a time in life to take a stand and I'm going to be proactive."

Pauline knitted something rectangular. She worked the wool vigorously. Gordon stretched his long legs under the table and laced his fingers behind his head. He hummed softly. Suzanne envied his calm.

She closed her eyes, whirling back.

By the time they had ordered number five on the menu, Wilma was slurring sentimental.

"My kid was a child once. A little child, y'know. He'd dance. You'd say 'Fancy steppin' and the little bugger would kick his legs up like he was at the goddamn Highland Games. Why can't they stay lil' n' cute? They get horrible, acne and, oh God, and disappointing and he had blond hair y'know, the lil' shrimp."

Suzanne feigned interest. The booze had dampened her mood. She slammed her fist on the next cocktail pictured in the game, a lychee martini. "Libations guy! A lychee martini!"

The bartender, trying to ignore the two inebriates by watching a football game on a small television in a nearby storage room, had had enough. He stormed over.

"A what?"

"A mai tai leech!"

The game would end. Around the World had tested his skill to the limit.

"Beer or nothing," he said.

A few businessmen who had stopped by for a quick drink piped up. "Don't give those broads any more!"

"Sir, I demand what's on this menu," said Suzanne.

She pried her eyes open and back to the meeting room. The fluorescent lighting sizzled. She propped her head, a rotten melon, in her hands. Her chest burned with acid.

The rest of the evening had lurched and shifted. Indignation and a tearful repentance. Staggering to the ladies' room. Pleading with the bartender. Searching for Wilma. Collapsing into someone's arms and being taken to a storage room. An ancient tongue, his mouth a crevice. Reptilian hands. A blonde delivering a newscast. The instinct to stumble away. And then, pale morning light and the apartment ceiling pressing down. Not the *bartender*?

Leslie fixed on Suzanne, his eyes two hard-boiled eggs. "If you don't care about the future, that's your business. I do. I am a professional."

She huffed and massaged her temples. Why was she antago-
nizing him, this man she saw three times a year? She took in
Pauline and Gordon. What was this weird menagerie? The two
occasions when the writers did mingle outside work were at
"team-building" potluck suppers hosted by Frank. At the last
potluck dinner, Leslie, instructed to bring dessert, had whipped
up *mille-feuille*. Pauline brought a beef stew and her knitting
needles. Gordon arrived with an earthenware vessel containing
burbling macaroni and cheese. Suzanne was an hour late. Toting
a case of beer and potato chips, she plopped the case on the
kitchen table and searched for a beer among the rattling empties.

Frank had banished his children to the basement so his co-
workers could have adult time, but the children kept running up
the stairs, begging to watch something other than ABS programming. Ten minutes in with the adults and the children raced back
to the basement.

The co-workers' conversation went from stilted to tongue-
tied. Suzanne, flushed from several beers, enthused over
Gordon's dish.

"What did you use, three or four different cheeses? Blue?
Gouda? And that was table cream in there, wasn't it? No low-fat
bullshit for you! No sir. I can tell you're a man who lives life.
You don't measure it out in increments. You don't ration pleasure, like some measly reward for having the fortitude to endure
boredom. Your medley of cheese is a revelation."

Flustered, Pauline and Leslie gravitated toward the kitchen,
where they washed their dishes and then looked around the
kitchen for more dishes to wash. Frank stormed down the basement stairs when he heard the opening bars of the theme song to
a forbidden television show.

Suzanne went out on Frank's deck and joined Gordon, who
watched the setting sun.

"So, you liked my macaroni and cheese?" he said.

She felt aroused by his attention. Of all the Canadians from
the west she had met, which weren't many due to all the
migrants from Ontario and Quebec, it was Gordon who fuelled
her fantasies. Tough yet earnest. Outdoorsy yet cultured. She

guessed he even voted Liberal. His effortless good looks, his tou-sled brown hair, wide smile, hazel eyes, tall and almost lanky physique appealed to her.

"Yes. Loved it."

Frank slid the screen door open and came outside, yawning. "It's getting late."

"It's nine o'clock," said Suzanne.

"Yeah, I know. Thanks for coming tonight, guys. Let's do it again."

They had never done it again.

Now, Suzanne stared at the vein that ran down Pauline's jawline. Prominent today.

"Is there any coffee?"

"No more coffee, either," Frank grumbled.

"Fuck!" Suzanne clenched her jaw to grind her teeth. Her hands made fists. The blood vessels in her head demanded constriction.

"Have some water," said Gordon. He offered her a sip from the mason jar he used as a glass.

"Water?"

His shoulder grazed hers. His clothes smelled of pine needles. Suzanne snatched the jar and swigged. Gordon probably bottled the water himself from some source in the Rockies, after an all-day hike through valleys and alpine meadows. He could probably rattle off the names of wildflowers and insects too, probably even make tea from both. She took another sip. She liked the image of Gordon hiking the mountains. She sniffed him, and for an instant imagined him naked. She adjusted her T-shirt and hoodie, acrid body odour wafting.

Frank tapped his pen on the table. He had dark circles under his eyes, a new sign of stress.

"Okay guys. Let's just cool off. Suzanne, take a walk around the block or something."

"Out there? It's minus 20."

"Now."

Suzanne sneered and grabbed her parka. She opened the door and collided with a grey-clad torso.

"Oh! I'm sorry!" she said.

She looked up at a tower of grey and black. Two slate-blue eyes locked on her. He must have been six-foot-four, with broad shoulders, authoritative grey hair, a strong nose and a remarkably clear complexion. His shirt and jacket upscale casual, he had the relaxed yet imposing air of a man who got his way. She stepped back. On his heels was a shorter, younger man with streaked blond hair, also wearing a jacket.

John Brady, the grey tower, went over to Frank and shook his hand. "Hello, Frank. Please excuse our lateness and cancellations. We've been introducing Jason to the media and consulting with communications. It's been hectic."

Frank let the big man shake his hand. "No. That's okay. Good to finally meet face-to-face."

Leslie grinned inanely and looked childlike in an orange pullover. Pauline kept her head bent but gave John a demure glance. Gordon cracked his knuckles. Suzanne absorbed the formalities. To the left stood Jason with one hand casually placed in his pocket. He inspected the room and then inspected Suzanne.

"Hey," he said.

She took in his beady eyes and felt instant dislike. "Uh-huh."

She felt Jason do a quick scan of her unfriendly demeanour. She narrowed her eyes at him.

Frank motioned Suzanne to take a seat. She wasn't going anywhere.

He introduced the writers to John Brady and everyone settled in around the boardroom table. John sat at the head, a father surrounded by his children.

"Team ABS," began John, "I'd like to introduce you to Jason MacLeod. He will be the new face of ABS membership. He's young, energetic, connected. Things are going to change around here. We've been hired by ABS to maximize viewer revenues and lower expenses. Not-for-profit doesn't have to mean not-*for*-profit. We're here to fix the mess left by years of government neglect. Any questions?"

No one budged.

"Frank?"

Frank inhaled, was about to speak, but instead shook his head.

"I know I can't replace Lawrence," Jason said. "But I can improve on what he did. We need to attract a younger audience if we want this, uh, publicly funded television to survive."

"And that's a big *if*," said John.

"So I'll need your help. I need to be briefed on the basics—programs, the merchandise we offer and any other related information."

Suzanne leaned toward Gordon. Pauline folded her arms. Suzanne knew Pauline had a serious academic side; her scripts were usually laden with words like "educational imperative" and "electronic distance-learning modules." ABS offered accredited courses in conjunction with programming, courses which in recent years had gone from "Pure and Applied Mathematics" to "Madonna: Post-modern Feminist Icon." This further slide into laxness, coming from the very guardians of educational television, must have distressed Pauline.

"Well, what Lawrence did," Frank said, "was to watch all the programming aired during the campaign, for his own information."

"I'm not expected to watch all the programming on ABS, am I?" Jason asked.

"No, you're not," said John. "That's what Lawrence did. All you need is a synopsis of the shows. The writers can supply that. And as far as the writing goes . . ."

Five bodies leaned in.

"We're going to phase it out. I mean, scripting what the membership host says is ridiculous."

Suzanne ground her molars. Her hangover had evaporated into churning fear. Leslie stroked what little chin he had.

"How is it ridiculous?" Frank countered.

"A host should be able to ad lib from notes. Do you think the viewers know that these breaks are fully scripted? They'd be appalled."

"But we craft a message," said Pauline.

"Maybe," said John, "but the message should come from personal conviction."

"Am I expected to have personal convictions?" Jason asked.

"Don't worry, Jason. Look, we need to save money. This is one area where I see redundancies. I welcome you to try and convince me otherwise. But we have to lose our stodgy image or risk total irrelevance. Am I clear?"

Gordon turned to Suzanne and mouthed the words *What the fuck?* Pauline cleared her throat. Frank doodled in his notebook.

"Now tell me about these so-called 'premiums' we offer viewers."

Frank brightened. He had a peculiar delight around the premiums. He rose from his chair. "Well, these are gifts we offer viewers who pledge certain amounts." He wheeled a cart heavy with toys, books and T-shirts toward John. "It's our way of showing appreciation for viewer donations."

John leaned over and plucked a stuffed toy from the pile. "What's this?"

"Oh, that's Rooey," said Frank. "He's an ABS favourite. Our very own kids' star. He can be had for a pledge of one hundred and fifty dollars."

John handled the object. A big blue football-shaped head dominated a small beige body. Tiny flippers represented limbs. The head had eyes sewn on, large black circles against glossy white almond shapes. Rooey's red mouth curled in a zealous grin. It was no secret that everyone at ABS thought Rooey grotesque. Inexplicably, Rooey survived. Very young children didn't seem to mind him.

"*Rooey's Playschool Adventures* has been an ABS success story. We've sold the show to over seven countries. He teaches kids about the world," said Frank.

"And he instills values," Pauline said.

John passed Rooey over to Jason. Jason laughed, grabbed Rooey by the head and threw him across the room. "I'm sorry!" Jason giggled. "I just had to. Sorry, that was inappropriate." He burst into more laughter.

John appeared to struggle at remaining serious. He glanced over at Jason. "Okay, no more tossing Rooey like a football."

Aghast, Frank gripped the arms of his chair. Suzanne almost smiled herself, but pulled back from the temptation. Jason lost his grin and quieted.

John laced his fingers. "Guys, I'm not going to let my opinion of your in-house productions get in the way, no matter how embarrassing or amateurish I think your shows are. Programming changes will come, but that's another meeting. In the meantime, we need to focus on the upcoming February campaign drive. I want it entertaining."

Suzanne tapped Gordon on the arm. "There's that word again."

"What do I mean by entertaining?" he said, as Pauline went to speak. "I mean story arc. Raising money is an inherently dramatic activity. Goals are set, and within a limited amount of time they need to be reached. Will we make it? Will ABS last another year? Will we be able to buy that new British series? Results hinge on viewer involvement. It's not enough to bludgeon them with the phone number to call to make a donation. I want these membership pledge breaks to be as dramatic as the programming itself. *Will we make it?* What could be more of a nail-biter?"

"I'm an actor by training," added Jason, "I can transmit feeling."

"I wonder what else he transmits," Suzanne whispered to Gordon.

"Tell you what," said John, regarding his membership team. "Whoever writes the most dramatic membership script—dramatic in a tension-filled sense—gets to stay on the next membership campaign. There's some fire for your bellies."

Frank looked puzzled. Pauline picked at her nails. Leslie gazed and blinked at John. Gordon leaned back and crossed his arms. Suzanne internalized the news by staring hard at the table, into the veneered grain, until her vision blurred.

John glanced at each writer.

"Keep in mind that I'm entering these membership pledge breaks into the Gemini Awards. If you don't know what those are, they're like Canadian Emmy Awards. For television programming."

"Oh, you can't be serious." said Frank.

"It's considered CanCon, fair game," said John. "Now everybody please consult with Frank about your scripting deadlines. The February campaign fast approaches. Our viewer revenue has to be more substantial. So I've given us an ambitious goal this campaign. We're aiming to raise one million dollars."

The writers' eyes bulged.

John rose from the table, with Jason following suit. He smiled. "It's not as impossible as it sounds. And if anyone needs anything, if you want to talk or if you have any questions, my door is open. Onto Marika and reception. Whose door is closed. That's it. We're done."

Having nothing to gather, John and Jason left the room.

Nobody spoke. The team sat silent, each person immobilized by the onslaught of managerial change. The fluorescent lights flickered overhead, the meeting room as sombre as a death row chamber. Suzanne glanced over at Rooey, who lay face down, mocked and scorned. Pauline put her head in her hands and let a couple of tears fall.

Frank growled. He stood up, went over to the door and stuck his head out, looking to see if the coast was clear. He then turned to his crestfallen colleagues, carefully shut the door and let loose a torrent of expletives.

Chapter 4—Secret 1, Secret 2 and Secret 3

She opened the door to the reek of sour urine. Lying on the steps of the apartment vestibule was the Newfie, so dubbed by the building's superintendent. Suzanne hated to call him using this all-purpose slur, so in deference to his inherent dignity as a human being and as a Canadian, she called the itinerant alcoholic the Fellow from Newfoundland. The super had chased the Fellow away a few times, but he'd come back, for some reason preferring to loiter in this small old vestibule instead of other vestibules and lobbies in the downtown core. She lived in one of Edmonton's rare brick apartment buildings just off Jasper Avenue, a three-storey circa 1935 walk-up. She had outgrown her insistence on "character" but was too listless to find another place to live. So shadowy neighbours and homeless drunkards it would be, until the dingy sadness pushed her over the edge.

She closed the door quickly, the arctic winter evening blowing in snow. She acknowledged the Fellow with a nod and then stepped over him to check her mailbox. She pulled out a few advertisements for 2–for-1 pizza and Chinese food. A while back she'd received junk mail for funeral services, brochures that asked, "Do You Think You're Prepared?" Emotionally she had been preparing to die for many years, on some days felt close to dead, but financially she had not begun to order her affairs. She thought she'd choose someone randomly from the phone book as her next of kin. She imagined the chosen person's confusion over the responsibility for the corpse. "Who? What? When? How much?" She had gone as far as deciding to be buried in a coffin. She liked to be supine in life, why not in death?

"Well, at least it's not ads hoping I'll die soon," she said.

The Fellow stirred a bit, dragging from a bottle of wine. Instinctively she checked the label. *Entre-Deux-Mers*. Not bad, not bad at all. Where did he get this? Some days she had to resist joining him, lolling on the steps and imbibing to oblivion. Tonight would be exceptionally difficult. The ABS meeting and its cruelty had left her exhausted. She tried not to look at the Fellow, at his matted grey hair, cracked red face and bloodshot eyes. She could crouch beside him and swig from the bottle. Laugh and get to know him. Find out why he left "the Rock" for the deserted city streets of Edmonton. Drink herself into a prehistoric time, become an amoeba, anything to rid herself of an essential loneliness.

She unlocked the door leading to the apartments. The vestibule windowpanes let heat escape. The Fellow sat close to the old radiator, an Eskimos bomber jacket and torn running shoes his defence against the frigid temperature. His crusty hands clutched the bottle. He smiled to himself, his teeth crooked and yellow, his breath putrid.

He couldn't stay in the vestibule overnight. He might get frostbite. "Hey . . . Mister . . . Fellow," she said, "come in here."

She held the door open for him. He struggled to push himself off the floor. Suzanne outstretched her hand.

"Grab my hand. Hurry."

He rolled on his side and reached for her hand. She grabbed his hand and yanked hard.

"Ahhh!"

"Sorry. Sorry. Sorry! Just crawl!"

He crawled up the four steps and into the hallway. She lifted him to his feet and leaned him against the wall.

"Go down to the laundry room in the basement and stay out of sight. You should be warm enough."

He smiled vacantly and weaved in place. He put his fingers to his lips. "Sssshhhhhhh."

She held him upright and led him down the stairs. She flicked on the lights in the laundry room and pointed under a long table.

"Under there. Stay out of sight."

She jogged up the stairs and heard his voice. Words reminiscent of a thank-you.

After a meal of rice and beans, Suzanne contemplated the telephone. At times like this, painful, panicky times when she felt like an eel wiggling through black unfathomable depths, a conversation with her one and only usually brought some relief. Eagerly, she pressed the receiver to her mouth.

"*Oui?*"

"Hey, freak!" said Suzanne.

"Hey, loser!" said Jackie.

"What's new in Montreal?"

"Our rent's going up."

"No."

"Yeah, after nine years Madame Boudreau has decided to start charging us market value."

Jackie Johnson. Suzanne's best friend since grade two. The mother, father, sister, brother, lover she never had. If Jackie had been male, Suzanne's life would have been a constant rapture. Suzanne tried to talk herself into expressing her love for Jackie through a sexual relationship, but imagining them naked together brought no pleasure, only the desire for comparison.

"Have enough money to cover things?"

"Yeah. Martin took another shift at the warehouse and I'm stepping it up to five days a week at the office."

"You gonna have time to paint?"

"I'll make time. Won't be as prolific, but we gotta do something."

Jackie was a visual artist who managed to make some money from her creativity, not enough to pay tax, but enough to claim professionalism. She had a day job and worked hard, never considering the granting agencies so many of her contemporaries leaned on. It was one of the things Suzanne admired most about Jackie. That, and her paintings of tornadoes. She celebrated nature's wrath.

"What about you?" asked Jackie.

"Some new bastards at ABS are shaking things up. They've taken over the network. They're all about the bottom line. The little one, Jason, I think I hate him."

"You'll figure it out. You always do. Meet any men recently?"

She wouldn't tell Jackie about the bartender and his lizard tongue. But she would tell her about a specific ray of sunshine that, until now, she'd kept under wraps.

"Not a man so much as a young man."

"Do tell."

"It's in the early stages. I'm confused, Jack. About generalities. Like the direction of my life."

"I'm sure everything will be fine. Like always. You land on your feet, all the time. Feet, knees, hands, face, et cetera."

Suzanne depended on Jackie's voice, soul and being. She pressed the receiver hard against her ear, hoping to feel Jackie's breath. She would dream about Jackie, and more than once Jackie had confirmed an incident or plan that Suzanne had dreamed weeks earlier. At some time in their adolescence, energy had transferred between them, an electromagnetic force, an exchange of cells, a splicing of nerve and synapse. Their voices were similar in tone and inflection. Jackie stood six inches taller, which came in handy for the many times she stood in as Suzanne's bodyguard. Are you sisters? people asked. Jackie had moved on, though, beyond the passion and anger of youth. She'd found a mate and settled down into a life of grateful routine and reward. Suzanne feared her devotion to Jackie, however true, was misplaced.

"Something's afoot, Jack. Nothing less than a paradigm shift. My job is threatened. How can I make myself obsolete-proof? I'm thirty-eight years old. There's an entire army of evil out there, ready to overthrow civilization."

"Lay off reading *Harper's* for a while," said Jackie. "And civilization was overthrown in 1980. Remember? The Sex Pistols Ladies Auxiliary?"

"Oh, yeah. I forgot about that. Our picnics in the park. Crustless sandwiches and airplane glue." Suzanne sighed. "I feel weird. When are you coming to see me?"

"You know we can't afford it. Why don't you come to Montreal?"

Suzanne had no reason not to visit. She had some money. A spinster aunt who always believed Suzanne odd and pitiful had left her a modest inheritance. In addition to the pittance Suzanne allotted herself monthly from her own savings, she topped up the amount with a stipend from the bequest, enough to keep her in booze and food and free to mope. After this next ABS membership campaign she'd be unencumbered for three months. She'd mooch around, bother shopkeepers in the neighbourhood with chat, brood at the library and feel discombobulated if someone sat in her "lucky" reading chair by the general stacks on the second floor. Self-employment agreed with her.

"What's your latest painting?" Suzanne asked.

"I haven't worked on a canvas in two months."

"Why?"

"Because I need a break. It will come, just not right now."

Suzanne lived through Jackie's steady output of work. One of them had to realize their potential. She willed all her vivid imaginings into Jackie's mind. Her dreams were telepathically made manifest through Jackie's visual talents, Bosch nightmares for the new age. No wonder she felt a little more off than usual lately. Jackie had stopped painting.

"Don't get on my case about not painting. I have other things going on."

"Like what?"

"Never you mind. I can't say right now."

"Can't say? What the hell?"

Jackie's voice went soft. "Foley. One more thing."

"What?"

"Something I saw in the *Gazette*."

Suzanne made a fist. Any news now that appeared in the *Montreal Gazette* that concerned them was never good.

"Yeah."

"I just think you might want to know."

"Did someone else die?"

Over the years, the old neighbourhood had seen three suicides and one murder. Suzanne and Jackie had survived their youth and the street by fortifying themselves with drugs and alcohol. Suzanne had made it to university on a partial scholarship but dropped out after a year. She became an autodidact, absorbing everything she could through a haze of pot and alcohol consumption. Jackie had picked up a paint brush as a kid and never put it down.

"Do you remember that perv who lived at the corner of Girouard and Sherbooke?"

Suzanne picked at eczema on her hands. "What perv?"

"That perv. You know, the one we all knew about. Pervert Audi."

The name shot through Suzanne like a bullet. "Oh yeah, that motherandchildfucker. I think the politically correct term for them now is 'pedophile.'"

"He got taken away. Last week. *Last week*."

She stared into her kitchen, a narrow room with a small window, devoid of any nourishment. "You say anything?"

"No. You?"

"No." Suzanne's heart pounded. "Wonder who squealed?"

"I think the term for squealing these days is 'therapy,'" said Jackie. "You still going?"

"Haven't graced a shrink's office with my presence in years. I'm through. What's done is done."

"You think?"

Suzanne snarled out the words. "Sure. I have mixed feelings. That's all."

"Fuck, eh? Fuckin' neighbourhood. Glad it's changed. For little kids now. Anyway, thought I'd tell you. Go out and see your new man, huh?"

Jackie always had sound advice. Suzanne hung up the phone and decided that's exactly what she'd do. She'd *do* something. She'd see the new young man. She liked younger men. They made her feel safe.

Heart labouring like a rusty pump, she slid her coat on.

Audi.

She shook her head. The memories caught in her mind like a television show.

On the set, a blond boy and a dark-haired girl, both ten years old and a bald man laughing.

She blinked. She could switch off the television show, she decided. No need to watch any more. She had enough to deal with in the present. *What's done is done.*

Click.

CHAPTER 5—COLIN

Suzanne shuffled in the frigid night air and looked at her watch: 10:20 P.M. He'd be finished by now, the last of the products stacked, wandering customers shown the door, cash registers emptied. He mentioned something about a new mop and how efficiently it cleaned spills in the aisles. It didn't take much to make him glad. She crossed the windy parking lot and waited outside the entrance. They called this a box store. A cluster of box stores was called a power centre, he had told her one night while they lay on her bed fully clothed. The Home Depot reigned supreme in the home improvement/renovation/hardware world, pushing out venerable retailers like Canadian Tire.

"You can't halt progress," he had insisted, while she caressed the back of his neck.

A month in, and they still had not been naked with each other.

Suzanne had gone into the Home Depot for light bulbs, wondering if they had any of the full-spectrum bulbs that supposedly alleviated depression, according to the free health magazines she'd pick up at the library. Once inside the massive warehouse she'd immediately felt depleted. Shelving twenty feet high, orange signs that screamed pricing, aisle upon broad aisle of every appliance, tool, paint, wood, home-related product imaginable, frequent barking on the PA system for customer service. She needed help. First, she would have to find help. She turned down an aisle and spotted someone in an orange apron.

"Excuse me," she said.

He fumbled the hair traps he was hanging. "Yes, miss?" Points scored. He called her *miss*. "Could you please tell me where I might find light bulbs?"

He wiped his hands on his apron, straightened and turned to face her. Light-green eyes complemented a smooth rosy complexion. His open countenance exuded goodness. He tucked his straight blond hair behind his ears. He stood a few inches taller than her, just enough to make body contact comfortable. He smiled.

"I would be happy to help you."

She began dropping by the store and joking with him. She impressed him with her job at a television station. He'd listen to her with adoration in his eyes. She started waiting for him after work. They'd go out for tea, or Colin would watch Suzanne have a couple of pints at whatever bar was nearby. One night she reached for his hand and held it. His eyes shone. The thought of his sweet smile and bashful shrugs made her hunger. After his shift one night she took him behind a dumpster. Pressing herself against him, she kissed him tenderly, over and over again, grazing her lips with his. She wondered if he had told his co-workers about her, the lady who hangs around the paint department. She imagined their conversations.

"I hear older women can fuck forever!"

"Aren't they wrinkly, though. *Down there?*"

Colin would jump in. "Gentlemen. I think the lady just enjoys looking at the colour palettes. Maybe she admires shades like Tradewind or Latte."

She scuffed at a snowbank. The frosty late-November air could induce psychosis in a vulnerable person. She pulled her toque lower on her forehead. She didn't mind wearing hats. Hats in this climate were a matter of life or death, as any drunk dumped at the edge of a prairie town by the police could attest. Hats made a difference. They gained a person valuable minutes in the cold.

The huge neon sign overhead hummed in the deserted night, the sky black, stretched over a concrete sea. It made her unaccountably horny, achy to the core. She sighed, her breath sweet from rum and coke.

Home Depot staff trickled out the door. She heard their laughter and good-natured ribbing. "Have a good one," they shouted to each other. Suzanne wished she could say things like "Have a good one" and not feel fraudulent. She envied their camaraderie.

Colin appeared, zipping his coat and flipping up his hood. He smiled at seeing her. He kissed her, his warm, full lips soft on her cold, chapped mouth. He smelled of wood chips and hot-dogs. He grinned, his eyes sparkling. Her groin tingled while her stomach clenched.

"Hey."

She wasn't Mr. Audi. No way.

Chapter 6—Manoeuvre #1

The next evening, Suzanne stared out her apartment window at a teen in a leather bomber jacket and running shoes negotiating blizzard conditions. He turned his back to the fierce battering wind and walked backward. A sharp maternal urge stabbed. *He shouldn't be outside on a night like tonight.* Drawing away, she finished a beer and mulled over a strategy.

Once again, nothing sexual with Colin had transpired the night before. They'd gone to a pub on Jasper Avenue, where Suzanne convinced Colin to have something to drink. She ordered him a draft beer, which he sipped daintily.

"I don't like the taste of this," he said.

"Nobody drinks for the taste."

"Sure they do. My parents do."

"Your parents are highly unusual."

He complained about nausea and sleepiness, then tested her patience with his smiles and giggles. But one day his giggles would become breath against her shoulder, hands cupping her breasts, his body consuming hers.

She sighed.

She knew she couldn't do it alone. Saving her job and her ass required the co-operation of the others. She pondered the freelance writer contact sheet on her desk. She could phone Pauline, but something about calling Pauline made her feel weird. Suzanne imagined she and Pauline held things in common. They were both unmarried and childless, and, on occasion, filled with a longing to be touched. An unintelligible guilt rolled through her.

Gordon? A similar nervousness shot through her, this time more acutely. A certain excitement. She visualized him doing various activities: shovelling the snow, enjoying a beer at a pub with his friends, showering. The idea of calling him made her giddy.

Leslie leaped to mind. She could call him. He didn't conjure up any feeling other than mild disdain. She rummaged through the top drawer of her desk. A year ago he'd handed out business cards at a production meeting. She fished through bills, hair, elastics, gum, AA pamphlets and stray pills until she found it— LESLIE ROZANSKI: WRITER, ACTOR, BON VIVANT—with his caricature embossed on the top left. He had not wanted his name and phone number on the ABS contact sheet. She stared at his home phone number. Phoning Leslie seemed logical. Business was business. She dialled his number and gripped the receiver, feeling like she had a gun to her head.

"Good evening."

Good evening? "Hi, is this Leslie?"

"Yes, it is."

"Leslie. It's Suzanne Foley from work. How are you?"

From the other end a pause, and the meowing of cats in the background. "How did you get this number?"

"You gave out business cards at a meeting."

"To you?"

"Yes. Leslie, I'm calling you about work. Did I catch you at a bad time?"

He cleared his throat. "Well, I was just changing the cat litter."

"Okay, I'll make it brief. We're going to lose our jobs if we don't do something about John Brady and his retinue."

"Retinue? There's just Jason."

"Jason is enough of a threat to be his own retinue."

He clucked, a tic of his that Suzanne detested. "And . . . ?"

"And we, the writers, should band together, to do battle."

"But whoever writes the best membership script gets to stay on," he said.

"Do you honestly believe that?"

"A Gemini Award is like an Emmy. He said so."

Suzanne sat at her desk and rested her forehead on the desktop. "Listen, Leslie. We're finished. We're all done if we don't thwart their scheme. Let's face it, we're unemployable anywhere else. Admit it."

"I will admit no such thing."

"All I'm asking you is to stick with us. Let's throw this membership campaign." She blurted out an addendum. "Please. It's all I have."

A cat let out a howl. "I am willing to forget we ever had this conversation if you promise never to call me again," he said.

Suzanne shook her head. She had miscalculated. Leslie didn't possess an iota of loyalty.

"You're right. I'm sorry. What am I thinking? What's done is done. Good luck on the scripting."

He offered a clipped goodbye and hung up, the cries of insistent cats the last thing she heard.

She sighed heavily and scratched a breast. One down, two to go. This "doing something" would take practice.

Chapter 7—Galaxyland

"I'm sure everything will work out," Colin said, unzipping his parka and taking off his mitts. Suzanne reached for his hand and held it. They kept their toques on, their faces still raw from razor winds. They strolled contentedly, quietly.

Sometimes the West Edmonton Mall was a good idea, usually on a blustery Monday evening when the consumer terminal was less populated. Shrieking teenaged girls congregated in clusters and tired mothers pulled recalcitrant toddlers. Packs of teenaged boys roamed the concourses, ridiculous in their gangsta bling bling. Once in a while, a duo of black-clad teenaged punks would pass, laughing at their own jokes, conspiring God knows what. She browsed the shop windows with Colin, feigning admiration for glittering necklaces and earrings. Suzanne fervently wished she could be a woman who loved nothing more than jewellery and shoes. Deep down, though, she just didn't give a shit.

"Would you like a pretty necklace like that?" Colin asked. He kissed her cheek.

The only time a man had bought her a necklace she'd thanked him, put it back in its box and returned it the next day to pay for an afternoon of boozing.

"Uh, I dunno."

Colin gently squeezed her hand. Being seen with her surrounded by his peers didn't seem to bother him. She did look young for her age, acted young, dressed young, but not young enough to pass for anyone who should be dating Colin. She never did tell him the truth about her age. He thought it was about twenty-nine. A nine-year age difference didn't matter to him, so why risk upsetting him with the truth?

Arms around each other, they strolled toward the indoor ice rink to catch a game between two rival Timbits teams, the history between the five-year-olds apparently tense, according to a frothing parent they had overheard in the mall. About to pass them, a square, blond-streaked man wearing a tan coat blew into his hands. Suzanne recognized him. Their eyes met. A split-second decision had to be made—ignore or acknowledge him?

He did a double take.

"I know you," said Jason. He stopped and turned around. "Melissa, right?"

She plastered on a smile. "No. Suzanne."

"Right. Sorry. At ABS. You're a—"

"That's right."

"Is this your son?"

Colin giggled. Suzanne glared at Jason. "No, and nice seeing you."

"Bully for you!" said Jason, giving Suzanne a little tap on the arm. "West Ed is great, man. See you at ABS. Keep up the good work. We should talk about the membership campaign sometime." He winked at her and continued on his way.

"That man is a boor." Suzanne scowled.

"Kinda jerky, I guess."

"A *nouveau* boor."

Shouts echoed in the mall. Boys whooped and jostled each other. Colin directed Suzanne away from the ruckus and down another wing of the shopping complex. "I have an idea," he said. "Let's go to Galaxyland."

"He's an idiot. Him and his fake blond hair. He looks like a second-rate porn star."

"What? Did you just say porn star?"

"Second-rate one at that."

Colin laughed, linked arms with Suzanne and steered her toward Galaxyland.

She squinted at a shopping mall directory where a small arrow pointed to a location on a map. *You are here.* In Edmonton, gateway to the end of the earth, and in Alberta, oil rich and crazy. *I am here.* Some days she wished Colin would tell her she was full of crap, to shut her up. He didn't. He either smiled or mooned over her, his green eyes a Yeats invocation: *"Come away, O human child! / To the waters and the wild / with a faery, hand in hand, / For the world's more full of weeping than you can understand."*

"Come on. The Drop of Doom will do you good," he said.

"I'm not going on the Drop of Doom."

"Oh yes you are!"

They approached the entrance of Galaxyland. Amusement rides clanked and screeched ahead. For all its dazzling convenience, Galaxyland lacked the elusive magic of an outdoor fair. The soft breeze of a summer night on shins dangling from a Ferris wheel, a wonderful gaze out into a starry sky this was not.

They bought ride tickets from a bored girl reading a magazine. The place was almost empty, except for a few clamouring adolescents. Parents corralled their children and steered them toward the exit so the big kids could take over. Suzanne looked up at the rafters. Good thing they hadn't stopped for pints beforehand.

They wormed their way to the Drop of Doom, a tower that released occupants of a cage in a free fall.

"All right!" He pumped his fist in the air. "Yeah!"

They climbed into a rickety cage and a greasy attendant strapped and locked them in.

"Is this safe?" she asked.

"Uh. Yeah. I guess," said the attendant.

The cage jerked forward.

"This isn't good, Colin. That guy guesses that this contraption is safe."

Colin reached over and slipped his hand on her breast.

"What are you doing?" she said.

"I'm ready now."

The cage rattled as it chugged along.

"Now? Colin. Wait."

The cage lunged onto a vertical track. Suddenly they shot up toward the rafters, every inch a heart-pounding bad trip.

"We can do it now," he said.

They jetted over Galaxyland, over people and twisting, undulating, whirling rides. She clutched the bars that pinned her. She wanted clarification.

"Hold on. Colin. Are you saying you're *consenting*?"

The cage came to an abrupt stop a couple of feet shy of the ceiling. Something made clicking sounds. He smiled, closed his eyes and touched her hand.

"I want to."

She couldn't close her eyes. She looked up at the ceiling. The cage slid forward and stopped.

"Wait. I don't want to free fall, Colin. I don't need the encouragement."

A loud buzzer sounded.

And they plunged.

Gravity drove screams from their lungs. She tasted her own beating heart. Instantly, Suzanne knew the sensation. The speeding cage scooped at the bottom and then rolled to a stop. Suzanne and Colin faced skyward.

"That was insane," he said. "I think I'm in love with you."

With every cell of her being alert to the out-of-body experience, she fought back another scream, this one decades overdue.

Suzanne rapped on Wilma's door, damning herself but not knowing what else to do. The evening at the West Ed had jarred her. The eleven o'clock news blared from behind the door. Finally she heard stirring and lumbering.

"Just a minute, for Christ's sake."

She heard wheezing. A pause, then locks and chains unfastened. Wilma stood in pajamas.

"Well, look what the cat dragged in. What the hell happened to you the other night?"

"Can I come in?"

"And it's nice to see you, too," said Wilma, "knocking on my door after eleven. You'd think you were my ex. By the way, did you let the Newfie in? He pissed on the first-floor landing and left his cock dangling from his pants. Old lady Chomsky on the second floor got the super to get rid of him. He chased him out with a shovel."

"Where's the Fellow gonna go? It's cold out there."

"When isn't it?"

"Got any alcohol?"

Wilma sighed and let Suzanne in. She went to the kitchen to get glasses. She plunked them on the coffee table and poured them each a shot of whisky. The television glowed with a local news report about a car crash on the Whitemud that sent two people to hospital with minor injuries.

"There goes car insurance," Wilma said.

"You don't have a car."

"But if I did, I'd be pissed."

Suzanne downed the shot of whisky. She never had acquired a liking or even an appreciation for hard liquor. It was strictly medicinal, unlike the staples of beer and wine.

"Look, I'm sorry to bother you. I know it's late and I'm . . . grateful for your company." Suzanne couldn't believe her own words.

Wilma curled up on the couch, giving Suzanne some room to sit. "What's the matter with you?" Wilma found the remote, lowered the sound on the TV and folded her arms over her gut. She looked cute in her pajamas, little hearts dotting the flannel. Comfort and hope in a cozy garment. She sipped her whisky, but then put it down. "You know what your problem is?" she stated. "You're too, I don't know. Something."

"You're not the first to say that. You barely know me."

"That's right. I try, but you just don't seem to, I dunno, relax or whatever. What do you want?"

"What do I want?" Suzanne indicated the bottle and Wilma shrugged. She poured herself another shot. She wanted to talk about the out-of-body experience she'd just had at West Ed, and how it reminded her of the time in her childhood when a man named Audi terrorized her.

"What do you mean, what do I want?"

"What do you want?"

"In general?"

Wilma sighed. "Now."

Suzanne gulped back whisky. "Right now?"

"Yes, for fuck's sake!"

"I'm sorry."

"That's all you ever say."

"I'm fifth-generation Canadian, I can't help it. I guess I just want company? Why don't we watch TV?"

"Watch it at your place."

Suzanne scratched her head. "Maybe I want to talk."

"About what? Come on, I have to work in the morning."

Suzanne poured herself another shot and downed it.

She saw the memory on the TV screen in her head. Audi handed Suzanne a glass of beer. She took a sip and shuddered. She swallowed it all, forcing back the skunky taste. Her friend Diana watched blankly, her shiny red lips moving silently. She dug in her purse and pulled out a pack of cigarettes. Mr. Audi sank on the couch beside Suzanne and put his arm around her.

"When are you gonna pose for pictures, like your friends? Don't you want to be a star?"

"I like waiting here."

Mr. Audi pulled out a little man doll. He had a weird expression on his face, like a dog that had been running.

"Watch this," said Mr. Audi.

He pressed a button on the back and the little doll man grew a penis. Suzanne knew what a penis was from her Grade 5 class. Diana and the blond boy with them giggled. Suzanne giggled too, clenching her fist. Mr. Audi put his hand on Suzanne's thigh. Squirming away, she went over to the TV and raised the volume.

"All right, you don't have to play," Mr. Audi said. He smiled at Diana and the boy and wagged his finger at them. "Come on, come on, let's have some fun!"

Diana stood up and tugged at her skirt. She picked a bug out of her hair and handed Suzanne her pack of cigarettes.

"Wait here," she said, "start on my homework."

The boy brushed by Suzanne and tried to grab her breast. Suzanne crossed her arms over her chest. She turned to watch Diana and the boy go down the dark hallway to Mr. Audi's bedroom, a hallway that seemed to go on forever.

Mr. Audi sat on the couch with Suzanne, undid her ponytail and stroked her hair. "You're a beautiful girl. If only you knew."

She wiped away the tears that ran down her cheeks.

He kissed her tenderly on the head and gave her a pen and writing pad. "Stay here, sweetheart. We won't be long. Write. You're good with words. Help Diana."

With the TV loud, Suzanne took Diana's homework out of her purse and completed her math and writing assignments while, fifteen feet away, Diana and the boy bent and splayed for the cold eye of a camera.

Could she tell Wilma that?

Time to change the channel.

Wilma was looking at Suzanne, waiting for her to say something. Then, she raised the volume on the TV. A weatherman predicted clear skies and the temperature rising to -20 for tomorrow.

"I'm sorry," said Suzanne. "This isn't fair. I know. You're my neighbour and I'm annoying you. I'm sorry."

Wilma lowered the volume a bit. "You know why I left the bar the other night? Because I had had enough. The bartender wasn't playing along, there were no men interested, we got a little loud and I thought, okay, time to go home. You? You kept saying that you had to 'see it through,' whatever the hell that means. Look, I wanna like you, Suzanne. Like you said, we're neighbours. Out here neighbours help neighbours. I don't know what the hell you do back east. Honestly, I feel sorry for you. That's it for tonight. Lighten up. I appreciate you wanting my company, but another time, okay, hon? I'm going to bed."

Wilma clicked off the television and rose from the couch. She shuffled sleepily toward her bedroom. She left Suzanne sitting on the couch, in the dark. Suzanne rose heavily, a gradual buzz taking hold. Wind whipped against the small living room window. She weaved in place, letting the room settle in her vision, cabinet and chairs anchoring her. It was time to go to her apartment and shut down for the night. She fixed on the bottle.

"Can I borrow the whisky?"

"No," said Wilma from the bedroom.

Suzanne stared at the bottle. She tucked it under her arm and groped her way to the front door. She turned the knob and stopped. She went back into the living room and returned the bottle to the coffee table and left.

Chapter 8—Pharmasave

Ten in the morning and the blue sky spread hope over Pharmasave. The skies over Toronto never spread hope. They were more of a pressing encasement. She could feel claustrophobic outdoors in Toronto. Suzanne crossed the street outside her building. Home on one corner, Pharmasave on another corner, and Teddy's, her favourite family restaurant, proximity and the absence of families its appeal, on the other. Her holy trinity.

It snowed overnight, fresh powder glittering on old snowbanks. Car exhaust rose in white plumes; the sidewalks and streets rang clear. She entered the pharmacy and observed a thread of snow whirling by her boots. She watched it dance. In winter all became vivid, God's design laid bare. She had an ongoing relationship with God, one that she struggled with due to compulsive reading and eviscerating doubt. She stepped over the little snow swirl, not wanting to disturb it.

Pharmasave, unlike Home Depot, housed products and services essential to well-being. Drugs. Vitamins. All the other stuff, optional. Suzanne moseyed down an aisle toward the prescriptions counter, passing various remedies and bulbous contraptions. She gawked at them and shuddered, hoping she would never have a need for a rectal syringe. Opium constipates. She remembered the story of an eighteenth-century writer and his chronic opium use. Toward the end of his life he either vegetated in a narcotic daze or begged friends to give him enemas to relieve his packed intestines. Would Gordon give her an enema if she asked? Frank? Leslie or Pauline? No, save it for John and Jason, give them the privilege. She caught herself drifting into unsavoury territory.

Suzanne drummed on the prescriptions counter. Manny was busy instructing a customer about medication. Manny was like a

loveable wisecracking bartender. He knew her. She felt valued
and appreciated here. He cared about her. He gave her good
advice, words to live by. Take NSAIDs with food. Take birth
control pills before bed. Do not operate heavy machinery while
on tranquillizers. Yes, he cared. He had finished with the
customer.

"Yo, bartender!" she said.

Manny scowled. "What can I do for you today? And don't
call me a bartender."

She produced a prescription from her jacket pocket. "I need
drugs. It says so on this piece of paper."

"It better not be written on a cocktail napkin, like last time."
He looked it over. "Ativan. Two milligrams?" He frowned at
her. "Were you in a car accident?"

"Why do people always ask me if I was in a car accident?"

"This is strong stuff."

"Well, I've had panic attacks lately. Dizziness. What's new
around here?"

He shook his head at the scrip. "Nothing much. Sabrina is
still on maternity leave. She'll be back soon."

"Already? Has nine months gone by already? How about
that."

"Give me ten minutes."

"Sure. So what else is new?"

Manny forced a smile and turned away from the counter.
"Ten minutes," he said with his back to her.

Once, on a slow day, Manny had talked at length about his
life in the former Yugoslavia. You have no clue, he said to her.
You were raised in this paradise. You were raised without hatred,
without history. You don't know from pogroms and ethnic
cleansing. He grimaced when she kept getting the Serbs and
Croats confused. No, she didn't know, didn't even know enough
about Canada's own history with indigenous peoples to offer a
parallel of some kind. She felt humbled by the tragic stories only
a countertop away. When Pierre Elliott Trudeau died some
months earlier, Suzanne had rushed to Pharmasave to buy a
newspaper. She fought back tears at the checkout counter as the

coins fell from her hands. Trudeau was more than a touchstone of her youth, more than a great Prime Minister—he was one of Montreal's true souls. Stifling a sob, she regarded the cashier. Guessing the South Asian woman was a new Canadian and eager to commiserate, Suzanne pointed at Trudeau's picture.

"So sad," Suzanne said. "The passing of Monsieur Trudeau." The cashier shrugged.

"Well, when you're dead, you're dead."

A little stunned by the woman's reply, Suzanne pressed on.

"Yes, he was a great Prime Minister, a citizen of the world."

"Well, when your number's up, that's it."

Disappointed by her remarks, Suzanne wiped away tears.

Crossing the street, clutching the newspaper, Suzanne had wondered what strife-ridden, war-torn hellhole the woman came from. What was the woman's story? What had she seen in her life or have handed down to her that would make her so callous? Was human life for her a commodity with death an everyday reality rather than a remote glitch in the plans? It took a few days, but eventually Suzanne found the woman's remarks very funny. Maybe she was a dyed-in-the-wool conservative and just hated Trudeau for the National Energy Program. This was Alberta, after all.

Now she glanced over at a blood pressure monitor and decided to kill some time checking hers. A panic attack had sent her to an emergency ward a couple of weeks earlier. While watching a violent, nonsensical movie at a downtown Cineplex, her feet had gone numb. After a few minutes the numbness had run up her legs, and her heart palpitated. Dolby THX sound shot around the theatre, gunfire ripping from every direction. Images cut from gun to explosion to bloodied people to fire. Her body in overdrive, she quietly left the cinema, hailed a cab and ever so calmly told the cab driver to get to a hospital in a hurry because she was having a heart attack. Panic attack, another hallmark of addiction, the pamphlets said. *Oh well.*

She slid into the seat, rolled up her sleeve and put her arm through the blood pressure mechanism. A cushioned strap slowly squeezed her arm, making her veins and arteries pulse. She watched with mild interest as the gauge flashed numbers. Suddenly, an image flared in her mind. Colin in the suicide cage. *I'm ready now.* Suzanne held her breath. Was he a virgin? The blood pressure reading beeped: 200 over 135.

"Miss Suzanne. Your prescription's ready," called Manny.

She stared at the blinking numbers. "Be right there. And don't worry about putting it in a bag."

CHAPTER 9—MANOEUVRE #2

She sat at a table in Earl's, a western restaurant chain decorated with brightly coloured papier-mâché parrots perched throughout. Pauline had hesitated over the phone, but agreed to meet. She thought Pauline had been crying.

Suzanne browsed the menu and its deep-fried offerings. No reason to be nervous, she thought. You're not on a date, if this is what it's like to be on a date. Surfacing at the Home Depot while Colin worked, skulking around after dark until he finished—she didn't consider that "dating." A date consisted of awkward silences over mediocre food at a middling restaurant. Her eyes rested on a menu item: *Fettuccini Alfredo with Shrimp and Red Peppers.* She closed the menu and signalled for a waiter.

"Can I have a pint of beer, please. Anything on tap."

"Will anyone be joining you?"

"Yes. Honest."

After pacing in her apartment, Suzanne had worked up the nerve to call Pauline. She'd felt preposterous pacing the cramped space. It reminded her of two fish she had in childhood. The fish lived out their days in a tiny aquarium, a starter kit no one ever bothered to upgrade. All day, every day, the fat fish and the skinny fish glided and moped. For five years—a remarkable life span for variants of goldfish bought as an afterthought by a neglectful parent—the fat fish grew fatter and the skinny fish darted quicker. Some nights she'd lie on the top bunk and stare at the fish, their silent presence a cloudy comfort. The fat fish sat opaquely on the aquarium gravel as the skinny fish dashed. The image insinuated itself until it morphed over the years into an antipathy to marriage. Suzanne, the skinny fish, darted in her apartment, hands on head, panicking and realizing the need to do something. There would be no fat fish to blame for inaction.

A knit scarf dangled in her peripheral vision. She looked up to see Pauline standing over her. Suzanne cleared her throat and indicated the chair across from her.

"Hi, Pauline. How nice of you to come. Please have a seat."

Suzanne cringed at her own formality. She couldn't help herself at times, having ingested too much *Masterpiece Theatre* in her early years. She'd sit catatonic in front of the family TV, older brothers and sisters roaming the streets and parents drunk in bed. PBS on UHF was one of the only channels the family received. Appropriate that she should be shilling for public television, where she learned about class systems, boarding schools and unattainable privilege. "I say, old chap, pass the tartar sauce, pip pip, jolly good, what," she'd say with an exaggerated British accent, amusing Jackie in grade school.

Pauline took a seat and placed her overstuffed bag on a chair. She removed her gloves and rubbed her hands together.

"Yeah. Cold, eh? What is it today, minus 21?" said Suzanne.

"It's minus 18. Warming up."

Pauline kept her coat on but removed her toque. Suzanne took a sip of beer and scrunched her toes. There would be no second beer, if she could help it.

"Have you ordered? The zucchini fingers are good," said Pauline.

"Ah. Yes."

"And the blooming onion."

"Right."

Pauline fingered her water glass. Suzanne looked up for some kind of divine inspiration. How to get the ball rolling?

Pauline ordered the spinach salad and Suzanne succumbed to her suggestion of zucchini fingers. Except for the wait staff and two other women dining, Pauline and Suzanne were alone. They avoided each other's eyes. Suzanne would be the first to snap under the strained silence.

"Thanks for coming today, Pauline. I just thought that maybe we should talk." Suzanne bit her lip and gnawed at it a while. "You know, this is awkward. The first time we've ever really chatted in what—"

"Three years," Pauline said.

"How long have you worked at ABS?"

"I've been at ABS for fourteen years. Even wrote for Rooey in his heyday."

"Rooey had a heyday?"

"You know his hair, the yellow tuft? I suggested it."

Pauline sipped her water. She was an ABS lifer. Any dismantling of the system would likely kill her.

"Yeah, that Rooey. Boy. The kids love him," said Suzanne.

Another uncomfortable lull.

"Look, uh, about the new regime at work. These people, they're, they're—"

"They're from Toronto is what they are," Pauline said.

Suzanne ignored the reflexive Toronto bashing. "Yeah. Now, things at membership have been okay. A grinding bore, sure, but okay. Do no harm. We have done no harm. We write scripts so that our fundraising host can ask viewers for donations. Not such a bad fate."

"Hear hear!"

"Right." Suzanne felt herself gearing up. "And now, now we're being taken over by people who think in terms of profit margins and budget cutting. Not that that is such a bad thing, when you look at it from their point of view." Desperation escalated. Suzanne felt defeated by her own ability to argue both sides of an issue, but continued.

"Look. They can't get rid of us. They can't just come in and tear down everything we've built all these years. They don't care about public television. And now they've pitted us against each other, for their own amusement. Who does John Brady think he is, a Roman emperor?"

"Probably."

"This won't do. Let's . . ." Suzanne forced the words. "Let's fight back."

Pauline reached for her bag. She pulled out some knitting needles and yarn. Suzanne didn't understand Pauline's fascination with knitting, but as far as nervous compulsions went, this one was harmless, much easier on the skin than obsessive hand washing.

"Fight back?" she said, resting the needles on the table, at the ready. "How?"

"By undermining that blockhead Jason. I don't trust him. Or like him, for that matter. Call it instinct."

Suzanne caught an image on a television over the bar. A CNN news story blared with a blond reporter doing a stand-up.

"See that guy?" Suzanne said, pointing at the television. "That's who will represent ABS. Some fake blond-haired guy out to make a buck any way he can. That's Jason."

Pauline turned in her chair and looked at the television screen. "No, it's not. That's some man on CNN."

Suzanne took a sip of beer. "Let's make Jason look so bad the network will beg to bring back Lawrence. We have to prove that membership can't be done on a shoestring."

"But it is done on a shoestring."

"It can't be done on any more of a shoestring. We must convince them that we're indispensable. They owe us more than shabby treatment and disrespect. Are you with me?"

Pauline picked at the spinach salad now in front of her. "You sound like Leslie."

"Leslie is only in this for himself. Are you with me?"

Pauline twiddled a fork. "I suppose I am with you, in spirit. What are you going to do?"

Suzanne leaned in. "It's what *we're* going to do. I saw you crying at the meeting. I felt like crying, but I don't know how to any more."

"You saw that?"

"Yeah. It hurts being told you're redundant."

Pauline chewed her greens. Suzanne blotted the grease off her zucchini fingers. They ate pensively.

"So, what will we do?" asked Pauline.

"Let's give Jason godawful scripts. Terrible. Full of lies. He won't know the difference. He's an idiot. Out of his depth."

Pauline looked at Suzanne. "It's embarrassing. You, having noticed me."

"I didn't notice so much as observe."

"You almost cried, you know. When Frank told us there'd be no more coffee. Your hands were shaking."

The two colleagues ate their lunch, the genesis of a bond forming.

Chapter 10—Happy New Year 2001

January in Edmonton. The Christmas holidays over and forgotten, the obligatory high spirits faked. She didn't fly back east to see anyone. Jackie and Martin sent the annual Christmas clown figurine gift, a garish porcelain lump with a pearl finish. The clown reclined with head propped in hand as though reposing under a willow in a park. *I am a relaxed clown.* Xs for eyes. They had passed it back and forth to each other over the years. It was Suzanne's turn to receive the clown. The Year of the Clown, 2001. Clown years were eventful years, the records proved. The last year she'd received the clown, bruises had started appearing on her legs. As amusing as she found exchanging the figurine, she feared what the clown would bring. Superstition started to play in her mind, a throwback to childhood days of kneeling in front of religious icons, praying for release. Out of perverse habit as a teenager she'd visit Mary Queen of the World Cathedral on what was Dorchester Street and sit transfixed by the votive candles glowing in front of different icons, prayers and petitions for health and peace, the faithful trying to slip in the back door by having Mary or Joseph intercede on their behalf. Jesus never struck Suzanne as the type who needed a referral first. God the Father she could see, but Jesus, that dreamy hobo? Such were the wonders of Catholicism and its elaborate rationalizations, her childhood religion still lying dormant, waiting to strike again. So she endowed the clown with powers it didn't have and fretted needlessly at its arrival.

She received a few holiday cards from acquaintances in Toronto, PR types who had her on their mailing lists. She stayed in Edmonton, upset that the library shut down for a couple of days. Pauline asked her if she would be visiting family.

"I . . . well . . ."

Suzanne paused. What would she say, what could she say? That both parents were dead, bodies turned to stone by drink. That her six brothers and sisters, one dead, one in jail, and the rest tucked away in varying degrees of suburbia across the country, were strangers by choice and circumstance, having never truly bonded except for sharing gallows humour and the joyless duty of weekly church attendance as a family. Why bring it up? So many nights of seeing her siblings flee the sickening heartache of inebriated parents for the tribal comforts of the street, and her young self a petri dish of quivering impression, left alone to watch her mother mutter to herself at the kitchen table and see her father unconscious on the living room floor. Her futile attempts to reach them with her child's love and the anguish of knowing that her parents were incapable of looking after their kids kept her still.

And in her parents' place, attention and gifts from Mr. Audi, who made her stomach hurt. Some nights, scrunched in a tattered armchair in a forgotten corner of the old basement, listening to drunken arguments from upstairs, she wanted to sacrifice herself, to give her parents peace. Her adult self wanted Audi dead, but the ten-year-old under the layers of years wanted to reach for that moist hand, someone who gave her attention.

"I . . . have plans . . . Hey, what are *you* doing?"

She kept a low profile on New Year's Eve. Wilma suggested she come along to the Nashville North for the Country Hoedown Countdown. "Just don't go slamming into anybody," she requested. Suzanne opted to stay in and watch an old war movie on ABS. She nursed a bottle of wine and lapsed into a comfortable self-pity.

Waking up New Year's Day, grateful for feeling low-level dread instead of crippling remorse, she took a stroll around the Alberta Legislature grounds. Minus 16 with the sky streaked grey and pink; the stark wintry landscape uplifted her. These landscapes reminded her of Glenn Gould. He understood and celebrated the essence of the north. Sometimes she dreamed of strolling arm in arm with Mr. Gould, both wearing layers of tweed and wool, rejoicing in a frozen world. She fantasized about him sexually, the possibility of shedding those layers and the hidden warmth of skin and tender exploration, of sharing a bed. Not possible. Number one—his mind was consumed by music and morbid introspection; and number two—he was dead. Her ideal man.

She heard from Colin a couple of times. He didn't invite her over to his parents' house for holiday cheer. He hadn't told them about his friendship with her, which suited her fine. So the holiday season passed without undue pain, a wash of lustrous depression glazing the days and nights. Buoyed by a stretch of clear skies and sunshine, she called Jackie and vowed to start the year fresh.

"I feel great. No more negativity. This year I keep an open mind. I will force the goodness out of me. I will do something! Maybe I'll even write a book, some chick lit thing. I feel like I have goals now. You know what I did for Christmas? I dropped by a shelter for dinner. Not to eat dinner, but to cook dinner. It's time to burst out of myself, before I asphyxiate."

"Uh-huh."

The February membership pledge campaign approaching, Suzanne sat at her desk and psyched herself to begin writing volumes of repetitive pleading. Fingers poised over the laptop keyboard, she typed a few words:

> *I hope you enjoyed this episode of* Detective Callaghan. *You'll have to wait until next week to see whodunit. Right now, we need you to do it! Get on the phone; dial 1-800-555-1212 with your membership pledge. Pledge 120, 100, 80, or 60 dollars.*

She stood and stretched. Two minutes in and already exhausted.

She couldn't believe the ABS hiring committee had bought the lies on her cv—the university degree, the years of steady employment in Toronto, the volunteer work with the Red Cross. She'd hoped they wouldn't phone her references; she kept Jackie on call for that. She was hired on the basis of her writing portfolio, three articles in a free entertainment weekly. Saying the word "Toronto" in the interview seemed to be enough. Suzanne didn't think of herself as a con. More of a personal spin doctor or an entrepreneur, if anything. Through osmosis she'd developed a deep caring for public television. It was for the people, and, whether she liked it or not, she was one of the people, born into the people.

She felt her heart wobble. Writing this drivel without the proper guidance of Frank seemed futile. Panic and numbing extremities occurred more frequently these days, their management becoming almost a daily chore. She reached for the Ativan on the bedside table and gulped a few pills.

Abandoning any notion of work, she carefully slipped on her coat and boots and left the apartment, searching for reassurance.

The worn beige carpeting a happy sight, she fought the urge to grin, but the Ativan won. She beamed, goofy and euphoric. The escalator to the library's second floor invited her to rise above it all. What crisis? What job? Books and magazines waited, many out of date. Mouth dry and rubbery, Suzanne licked her lips. If she could have salivated, she would have. Sanctuary unlike any bar or pub, she revered the library. She drifted toward the encyclopedias.

By the information desk a familiar-looking man perused the announcements on a community bulletin board. His blue Gore-Tex jacket and knit toque gave him away. Gordon. She smiled broadly, stupidly, feeling her heart flutter. *He went to the library too? He was one of them, one of her?* She watched him tear a strip of paper off an ad and put it in his pocket.

"Gordon!"

He turned, and she waved and walked toward him.

He grinned. "Hey."

"Hey. Hey you."

She smiled idiotically at him, gazing into his hazel eyes.

"Your eyes are kinda greenish."

"My eyes? I guess. They change colour now and then." He searched her eyes. "Yours are blue. Sort of a . . . milky blue. And red. Do you have allergies?"

She lowered her eyes. He made her warm. "No, no aller- allergies." Her words tumbled. "So, how were your holidays?"

"Nice. We went skiing in Jasper. Stayed at the Lodge. It's a little tradition with my family."

His family had traditions.

"What did you do?" he asked.

"Uh, I stayed in town. It's . . . a little tradition."

Suddenly, from the thick of the paperbacks, a young boy raced toward them. He plowed headfirst into Gordon's crotch.

"Boom!"

Gordon buckled. "Owwww! Geez. Hey buddy, watch it there."

The boy whooped and waved a book. "I found it! Tornadoes! Read all about them!"

"Ssshh, Ryan. Keep it down." Gordon smiled. She watched the boy spin around and flap the book.

"Who's this?" she asked.

"This is my son, Ryan. Ryan, this is Suzanne, someone I work with."

Ryan, a ball of a kid wearing an Oilers jersey, waved the book at her. "Hi!"

Gordon had a son, undeniably cute, just like his dad. She felt a twinge of disappointment. "Hi."

"Look! Do you like tornadoes?" Ryan asked.

The kid couldn't be all that bad. "Yeah, a lot. You're like a tornado yourself."

Ryan spun around.

"Okay Ryan, enough," said Gordon.

"How old is he?" she asked.

"Seven."

"Seven, eh? So, can he feed himself or what? What can kids do at seven?"

"I wish he could get a job. Maybe he could do my member- ship writing for me." Gordon put his gloves on. "Okay, Bud, let's get going. Mom's waiting."

Suzanne smiled wanly. Ryan fumbled with the zipper on his parka. Suzanne wanted to help him, but held back. That was his mom's job, making sure he was bundled up. Fed, housed, loved, nurtured. Their casual bumping into each other was drawing to a close. Gordon and Ryan would go off to a house somewhere and Mom. She'd have a stew warming on the stovetop, and a fire going. They'd eat, watch a little TV, read a few picture books, and then, once Ryan had washed up and brushed his teeth, they'd tuck the child into bed. Then Gordon and Missus Gordon would cuddle on the couch beneath a cozy blanket in front of the fire. Maybe have a half-glass of wine. They'd discuss their days, this day and the days to come. She probably had red hair, long and thick. They enjoyed each other's company. They skied together. Their sex life was still passionate.

Now gloomy, Suzanne watched Gordon help his son with the zipper. Then she remembered her meeting with Pauline, the fledgling membership union and the call to arms. She could get together with him for business reasons.

"Er, Gordon. I met with Pauline, about work. Uh, would you be interested in getting together to talk about membership and what we should do? About what's going on? About the future?"

He held onto Ryan, who flipped through the picture books. "Sure, if it helps. Name the time and I'll see if that's good for Ryan's mom."

"How about—" She stopped as she took in his words. She cleared her throat. "See if next Thursday is any good. Afternoon or night. Maybe night."

"Okay." Gordon pulled Ryan's hood over his head. They headed to the escalator. "Call me. See ya later."

Suzanne watched them descend. Just as they dropped out of sight, Ryan turned around and waved the tornado book.

Chapter 11—What They Need

Creaking stairs and the sound of bronchial distress outside her door alerted Suzanne. She checked her watch. Wilma, right on time, her shift finished. She needed an opinion on the Gordon situation, a question answered. Was Gordon married or separated from his wife? Although Suzanne hadn't answered Wilma's phone calls on a couple of recent occasions, she now desired her company.

Suzanne put down the plate of spaghetti she slurped and lowered the volume on the TV. She opened her door.

"Oh, hey Wilma," she said. "I thought I heard you! How's life?"

Wilma stopped and let the grocery bags she carried drop to the floor. Her short bleached-blond hair revealed dark roots. Her face sagged. Her eyes were puffy. She had applied her makeup lightly today, not the usual shellacking.

"Hey."

"Listen, what are you doing now? I gotta ask you something, if that's okay."

Wilma wheezed and looked at Suzanne sadly. "Sure. Come on over. Could you do me a favour, though? Could you take a couple of these bags?"

Suzanne went out into the hallway and grabbed the grocery bags. Wilma tinkered with a mound of keys and opened her front door, Suzanne trailing in. Wilma flicked on a light and shuffled into the living room. She found the TV remote and turned on the set. She eased herself on the couch and switched on a table light.

"I don't feel like making anything tonight. Think I'll order in. Do you want anything?"

"Where you ordering from?"

"I dunno. Maybe the Chinese guy." Her purse fell onto the floor from the couch, spilling most of its contents. Wilma cursed softly. "Fuck." She struggled to lean over and pick up the items.

"Have any beer or anything?"

"No beer. Or wine. Maybe there's something in the cupboard above the stove."

Suzanne stood on tiptoe on a chair, felt around a greasy shelf and found crème de menthe and Baileys. It would do. She poured herself a tumbler of Baileys.

"Do you want some?"

"No," said Wilma, reaching for a brush. "I need to lay off the hooch."

Suzanne pulled up an ottoman by the couch. Wilma settled back in, having collected her purse. Eyes absent, she flipped through TV channels. Suzanne choked down the Baileys, the sweetness revolting.

"Wilma, I need your opinion on something that's happened to me. Wilma, are you listening?"

Wilma lowered the volume on the remote. She looked at Suzanne, her expression weary. "Why haven't you answered your door when I've knocked?"

"You've knocked on my door? When?"

"About five times in the last couple of weeks. I know you're home, too."

Suzanne gripped the glass and put on her best clueless look. "When? How was I home?"

"Maybe you weren't home, I don't know. You might not like me and I might not like you, or understand you, or get you, but . . ." She sighed and ran her fingers through her hair.

"Mind if I turn on another light? It's dark in here." Suzanne switched on the other table lamp. She licked her glass and stared off at the cat figurines in the cabinet. She didn't spot her favourite figurine, a cat holding a mop.

"I got some bad news from the doctor," Wilma said, picking at her nails.

Suzanne scrunched her toes and frowned. "Where's the cat holding the mop? Is the cat holding or dancing with the mop?

I've never been sure. It isn't broken, is it? Didn't you get that in Hawaii or Jamaica or somewhere like that? I have a clown figurine. It's hilarious. The clown is reclining, sort of like it's posing for a centrefold."

"I have cancer," Wilma said.

"Cancer. Did you just say you have cancer?"

Wilma repeated herself, playing with a ring on her finger. "I have breast cancer."

Images of children jumping caught Suzanne's attention. She looked over Wilma's head at the TV. A grade-school class gathered around a beige thing with an enormous blue head. Rooey? Rooey was doing the circuit again, the appearance probably a tie-in with the membership campaign. This was being reported on a local commercial affiliate, a PR coup for someone at ABS. Suzanne looked back at Wilma. Wilma hugged a pillow and hung her head. Suzanne leafed through a *Women's World* magazine on the coffee table.

"That's not too good. Try not to get down about it."

Wilma raised her head. "Try not to get down about it? Are you *human*?"

Suzanne cleared her throat. "What I mean is . . ."

She searched her mind's database for sympathy. She'd have to excavate her heart for the proper response. Her heart, that blustery storm, that block of ice. For a person who worked with words, Suzanne was deeply inarticulate. At times she wondered if she was sentient at all. The word "psychopath" was once hurled at her by a frustrated high school teacher. A badge of honour at one time, the label now made her reflect.

"What I mean is that we live in a city with one of the best university hospitals in Canada, a pioneer in organ transplants, among other medical procedures. I'm confident that you'll receive the best care there is, and in a prompt manner. Breast cancer is treatable with radiation therapy, surgery, chemotherapy and medication, if I'm not mistaken. Unless you have a particularly virulent form of cancer, I'm sure your prognosis is good, if not excellent."

"They might lob off my tit," Wilma cried.

Suzanne paused. "Well, if mastectomy is indicated as the best course in your case, I'm sure your oncologist knows what he or she is doing. Is this just a biopsy or do you have to get a tumour removed?"

"Maybe the whole boob."

"Okay. Well, there are support groups for breast cancer survivors. I understand this must be difficult for you. If there's anything I can do for you, don't hesitate to call."

Amazed, Wilma stared at Suzanne. "You sound like one of those brochures in the waiting room at the hospital, for Christ's sake."

"I know. I'm sorry. I can't help myself." Suzanne got up and poured some more Baileys for herself and some for Wilma.

Wilma shrugged and took the glass. "Here I am, fifty-two years old. Why do I have cancer? Where did this come from?"

Suzanne lowered herself on the couch. She resisted reeling off the many probable reasons why Wilma had cancer: obesity, a lifetime consuming trans-fatty acids, excessive consumption of alcohol, a pack-a-day cigarette habit, a sedentary lifestyle.

"I don't know. So, what are you going to do?"

"What am I going to do? Die, maybe."

"You're not going to die."

"I'm tired. Tired and depressed. I'm better than I was a few weeks ago, when I was knocking on your door."

Suzanne scrunched her toes again. "What did you do then?"

"I called my son. 'There's no service for the number you have dialled.' Actually called the ex. He was genuinely concerned. Said he'd take me to the hospital, if I needed him to. Then he asked me for money. The fucker. I told a girl at work, told her to keep it quiet. I can't afford to lose my job. This really comes out of the blue. I'd been feeling tired for a while, but I didn't think anything of it." She slapped her thighs. "Well. What's done is done. No use crying over spilled milk, no pun intended. I'll take my lumps, no pun intended." She made herself laugh.

Suzanne smiled. "You'll be okay."

Wilma looked at Suzanne, blue eyes shining with tears, her eyeliner smudged.

Suzanne pushed the words out. "Do you want a hug?"

"That would be nice."

Suzanne reached over and put her arms around Wilma's thick torso. Wilma held on and quietly sobbed. Wilma felt soft and plump. Like a mother would, Suzanne guessed. She stared over at the firing television and let her go.

"If I need your help," Wilma sniffled, still holding Suzanne, "will you help me?"

"Of course," she said, squirming out of the embrace. "You can count on me."

Chapter 12 – A Heavenly Promise

They necked furiously in the last row of a Cineplex. Not one for public displays of affection, if they didn't include coitus and a snack afterward, Suzanne nevertheless allowed Colin to search her mouth with his tongue. He kissed with endless enthusiasm, rolling his tongue and sucking her breath. His hands never rose higher than her forearms, which he stroked briskly. Once in a while Suzanne gently eased him away, so she could wipe his saliva from her lips.

In the same row a short distance away, she caught a solo moviegoer staring at them. He leered, his face illuminated by the flickering images on the screen. Suzanne gave him the finger.

Colin kissed her and rubbed her thigh. Open-mouthed, lips full and glistening, he pulled her in.

"Colin," she whispered. "Hold on. Wait."

"I don't know if I can."

"Baby, please wait."

"You drive me crazy."

He bit her neck, which made her writhe. She'd have to put an end to this. She sighed and held his hand. "Calm down, son."

He stopped in mid-motion. "Did you just call me son?"

"You didn't hear that."

A couple finally glanced back and shushed them.

"I didn't mean it that way. Just that we can't, uh, we gotta calm down. Wait. Let's watch the movie."

Afterward, Suzanne and Colin sat in the Cineplex's neon café watching a popcorn machine burp corpulent puffs. Colin drank cola and chewed ice cubes. For the first time, she thought Colin felt awkward with her, maybe even mistrustful. She'd have to settle him down. Do something. The honourable thing would be to break it off and let the young man cavort with girls his own age. For many weeks they had been inseparable, going to movies, taking walks in the park, laughing about commercials they saw on TV or imitating people they saw on the street. But they had not consummated their relationship. As eager as she was, she hesitated. She gave him an out, as she had all previous boyfriends, of which there weren't many. Every few years, Suzanne collided with some ill-starred male who, through idiosyncrasy and ineptitude, made himself attractive to her, usually sex-starved bachelors too sensible to be misogynist but too insular to court companionship. She developed relationships with these men out of pity and the need for sexual release. Leaving presented no problem. They invariably understood.

Why, then, did she think about Gordon, by all accounts a well-adjusted male, and hope for a phone call? She pictured herself actually sitting *by* the phone. Gordon had become music she couldn't get out of her head, a Bach invention, as played by Mr. Gould. *Finger me, Glenn.* She looked back at Colin, his open face, and his sea-green eyes rippling with doubt. She'd have to distract him before he asked too many questions.

"Let's play air hockey!"

She steered him toward the games area and fed coins into an air hockey table. A glowing puck popped from a net. She pushed a paddle toward him.

"Prepare for some old-fashioned annihilation."

Suzanne placed her hand over the steady stream of air that buffered the table. She leaned in and banked the puck against the boards. It slammed into Colin's goal. He studied the table.

"Okay. I see."

"You're going down, my friend."

His turn. He smiled at her and then blasted the puck in a straight line, sinking it in her net.

"Oh. How about that?" he said.

She gawked. How could she have missed it? She hadn't prepared for something so simple. She knew his game now. Basic 101 air hockey. She wouldn't immediately destroy him. She'd put on the brakes halfway through the game and then roar back with two consecutive goals.

Warmth spread between her legs. She smacked the puck. It tore from side to side and broke into his zone. He lunged at it and fired back. She pounced and sliced it back at him, missing the slot by inches. They chopped at the puck, their play wild and intense. Heat and fury consumed her. Skin from her hand blistered as she gripped the paddle and swung at the puck over and over again. Colin's face betrayed no savagery. He focused on the puck with serious intent, ripping it at her with gentlemanly form. She missed blocking it and saw it drain into her goal.

"Hmm," he murmured.

Dumbstruck, she stared at him. How could this boy barely out of his teens beat her, the air hockey queen of downtown Montreal? Had she lost her touch? She'd once defeated a skinhead in a seven-to-six match. For a few days she'd felt like a legend in her neighbourhood, a scrawny stoner girl who'd triumphed over a skinhead. Briefly, the gangs at her high school had acknowledged her presence in the hallway. Those few days may have been the best of her life because she was no longer a weak little girl at anyone's mercy. But now, she was no longer queen of the arcade. What was she? Who was she?

Suzanne snarled and grabbed the paddle. She would win. And kill him.

But she didn't win. She couldn't keep up with Colin. Her mild-mannered young lover graciously trounced her. After the puck sank in her goal for the last time, she whipped the paddle at his head and kicked a nearby garbage can. A few arcade patrons noticed her outburst and laughed.

Colin suppressed a grin. He put his arms around her. "C'mon, Sugar Crisp."

She pushed him away but he came back and held her tight. She struggled against his embrace.

"Fuck off!"

"Come on. We're just having fun."

"Yeah. Fun."

Her eyes blazed. She turned her head so he wouldn't see. An image rushed. On a black-and-white TV set cartoons bounced.

Processed-cheese sandwiches were fanned on a green serving plate. The blond boy sat beside her on the couch, giggling nervously. Her stomach clenched. Diana lit a cigarette and wiggled her toes. Mr. Audi laughed and slid a magazine onto Suzanne's lap. There were pictures, gross pictures on the page. Mr. Audi said, "I love you."

Her stomach a lead bar, she wanted to punch Colin.

"So, what do you want to do?" he said.

I say, old chap, pass the tartar sauce. Suzanne wiped away tears. She'd pull herself together and blame some external force for her mood. She'd pin her tears on Wilma. Might gain her some sympathy, or perhaps even score her some physical consolation.

"Look," Suzanne said, hanging her head, "I've had a rough few days. I just found out that my neighbour Wilma has breast cancer. It's really making me sad. I feel terrible."

As predicted, Colin responded with tenderness. "Oh, darling. I didn't know. I'm so sorry. I'm so sorry you feel sad. Is there anything I can do to make you feel better?"

She raised her head. "I'll be okay. Just be with me, Colin."

He nuzzled her hair. "You know what you need right now? A beer. Let's go get you a beer. That always cheers you up. Would you like that?"

They ended up at her place, the only place for them to have privacy. Mollified by a couple of pints and Colin's tenderness, Suzanne relaxed into a faint benevolence. She apologized for her behaviour and for embarrassing him. She forgot about the sympathy ploy. She almost attempted to articulate what was in her heart, but the words caught in the strangulated canal that was her throat. His eyes made it all better, made her believe that the meek shall inherit the earth.

They lay on her bed gently kissing. She stroked his cheek. He'd forgiven her so much. He'd forgiven her for being her. Did he know that? A tear escaped and ran down her cheek.

"Hey," he whispered. "It's okay."

He kissed her tear. He reached for her hand and guided it down to his jeans and the bulge between his legs.

"Oh, Colin, I don't know," she whispered in his ear.

"I do. I'm ready."

She held his hands and pressed them to her chest. "I have to ask you something. When you say you're ready . . . does that mean you're *ready* ready?"

"I've never done this before."

"Are you sure?"

"Listen," he said. "I care about you. We have fun together. You excite me. I want to express my love for you."

A heavenly promise. A virgin. She gazed over at the snow crystals, infinitesimal light and water patterning the windowpane. She kissed him, their lips a cosmos.

"Sweetheart."

He sat up and pulled off his sweater. He lay beside her, his chest hair blond and sparse. She touched his skin, a gift she didn't deserve. She turned her head toward the windowpane and swallowed the dark thoughts and words that churned. *I wanna fuck your inner child.*

A party to his unveiling, her heart beat violently.

Chapter 13—Sturm Und Drang

She woke up thinking of Rooey. Who was responsible for that misshapen freak frolicking on a commercial station's newscast leading a preschool sing-along? There had been talk of new branding at ABS; the word "branding" had never been used at ABS before John Brady and Jason Macleod had been hired. Branding, that coercive implantation of logo and trademark, a hot stamp seared on the brain. She hated the sterile strategies of marketing. She hated Jason, who was his own brand.

Gazing out the window at a weak sun, tea mug in hand, she readied herself for several hours of writing pledge pleading. She stretched and groaned. Instead of feeling buoyed by her first lovemaking session with Colin, the intimacy had left her sluggish. While Colin had turned out to be a pleasant surprise in every way, she resented sharing herself. No man had ever spent the night with her. She booted them out as fast as she could. He hadn't protested when she had asked him to leave. He didn't know any better.

"Sure, dumpling. I'll get the bus."

"Do you want money for a cab?"

"No. Your love will keep me warm. Yes, I really did say that," he said, showing himself out.

Her groin aching from the sex workout, she resigned herself to the task at hand, begging people for money. At the very least, Canadian public television didn't interrupt the programming with pledge breaks, the way PBS did.

The phone rang. She looked at it for a while, then answered.

"Suzanne. It's Frank. How are you?"

". . . Fine?"

"Good. How goes the writing?"

"Uh, yeah, that's something I want to talk to you about—"

"Listen. John wants all the pledge writers to come in for Open House."

"Open House. Why?"

Frank cleared his throat. "He wants you all to come in to work it."

"Work it?"

"Yeah, greet people, explain what ABS does, kiss hands and shake babies, you know."

"But Frank, we've never had to go in before. We don't actually work in the building. We're freelancers. Independent contractors. Consultants."

"I know. But John wants you in anyway."

"Are we getting paid for this?"

Frank sighed. "No. You'll be volunteering, which in my mind is not an outlandish thing to do for the cause."

She frowned into the phone. "Involuntary volunteering. I'd like to have a choice in the matter. Do I?"

"Let's just say that if you don't volunteer, it won't look good to John."

She waved the receiver in disbelief and then barked into it. "This is ridiculous. You mean I have to stand around and look like I *belong*?"

"It's not so much to ask. If you're enthusiastic you may even get noticed."

"Frank, I can't believe you said that."

He lowered his voice. "What am I supposed to do? Do you think I like sucking this up? The man has no respect for me as is. It's depressing. Just do me a favour and come in. Please. For me."

Suzanne visualized the open house, the swarms of families and assorted do-gooders crowding into the two small television studios ABS barely maintained. The children with their sticky peanut butter fingers running amok on the set of the current affairs show *This Day in Alberta*. The questions—*How does TV work? Where's Rooey? How can I get on TV?*

"Do you really want me there?"

"Yes. This is my ship and we all go down together."

"Okay, Frank. But we may not be sunk yet."

She hung up and stared at her laptop. She'd play that thing like a Steinway and create music. *Sturm und Drang*. She'd give them drama. There would be weeping and gnashing of teeth.

Settling into her chair, fingers sweeping the keyboard's energy field, she started typing.

ABS MEMBERSHIP SCRIPT
SATURDAY FEBRUARY 22: BREAK #1
OUT OF: INSPECTOR CALLAGHAN
INTO: INSPECTOR HAWTHORNE
JASON: (Reacting to Inspector Callaghan, camera #1)
Why would anyone murder a child? (Jason shakes fists, raises eyes heavenward.) WHY!? (stops) Sure, we all think about it now and then—how nice it would be to rid ourselves of our whining, parasitical offspring—but to actually carry out such an insane act? I think it's time we brought back the death penalty. If only Inspector Callaghan would champion the cause of capital punishment. Get all of Britain to reconsider its justice system. But that's another show.

(Jason turns to Camera #2) You know what else is being killed? Public television. Educational non-commercial quality programming. (Jason rubs face with hands and rolls up his sleeves.) Look, people. This is not some idle threat, some fundraising scheme. (Jason raises his voice.) It's the TRUTH. You could very well be responsible for the obliteration of everything we hold dear in this country—democracy, freedom, peace, order and good government, if you don't pick up the phone, dial 1-800-555-1212, and donate as much as you can. Will the sky fall if you don't pledge 150 dollars, 120 dollars, or 100 dollars? Let's be honest. YES. Civilization will collapse, just like the Roman Empire, the Ottoman Empire, and the British Empire. That's right, you heard me, your beloved British Empire. Why? Because you didn't safeguard the public from the rotting influence of commercial television. The machines will rise, my friends, they will take over your communities, your streets, your way of life if you don't become an ABS member now with a donation of 100 dollars, 80 dollars, or 60 dollars.

You think you're safe in Grande Prairie or Camrose or Cold Lake? Think again!

The insidious spread of commercialization is like a necrotizing infection wasting your body and brain. Do you want to die? Keep watching those commercial programs that promote the seven deadly sins. But if you want to live, truly be free in a world that seeks to destroy the human spirit, save yourself now. Become an ABS member and join our fellowship with a pledge of 250 dollars, 200 dollars, or 180 dollars. Can't afford that much? Donate in installments and charge it to your credit card. Together, we can protect ourselves against the murder of intelligence in this province, just like Inspector Callaghan protects the citizens of Gloucester from evildoers. Don't be a murderer; call 1-800-555-1212 with your membership pledge. And now, Inspector Hawthorne.

She paused to review her handiwork; a thread of paranoia here, a stitch of evangelical Christian zeal there, all in all, a lovely brocade of lunatic ranting. She only had another hundred minutes of this to write. She'd dig into her unconscious and let the venom spew. She wouldn't have to dig far.

Chapter 14—Open House

People came to Open House to do something. Get out of the cold, let the kids run around, gorge on free snacks. The occasional hardcore ABS supporter would deluge a volunteer with esoteric questions about obscure programming, but for the most part the Open House served as a holding tank for excited, screaming children and their exhausted, grumpy parents. The majority of visitors didn't donate money to the organization. They saw print ads in the *Edmonton Journal* or *Edmonton Sun* and would decide to spend a Saturday afternoon hanging around a television station, the word "free" the biggest draw. No wonder Brady wanted as many hands on deck as he could find. The February membership campaign's goal, defying all reason, stayed at one million dollars. Short of canvassing door to door, ABS would have to wring as much money out of people as possible at events like Open House. Interesting them in the high-quality, commercial-free programming ABS aired, however, proved a gargantuan task. The only way to appeal to their better natures and support programming that didn't include sex, violence or anything American and popular was to exploit their fears about the well-being of their children. The tactic proved effective in pledge scripts.

Suzanne, Gordon and Pauline sat officiously behind a table on the second floor by the elevator, like electoral workers at a polling station.

"Support commercial-free programming. Support ABS," Gordon invited the passersby. "Anyone. Anyone?"

The ABS building, with its metal filing cabinets and ancient computers, inspired nobody except managers to cheat on their expense accounts. Suzanne rapped a pen against the membership forms in front of her, thinking how anything creative ever blossoming in oppressive environments—be it garbage-strewn ghettos or stale, blanched offices—was considerable evidence for the existence of God.

Marika walked by holding a balloon bouquet. She wore an ABS T-shirt with the slogan "ABS: Your Television Broadcaster" in bright, fat orange letters. The ABS logo, a circle with a line through it, emblazoned the back. How the circle with the line signified the spirit of television inflamed debate every few years, which quickly petered out. Suzanne and Gordon both refused to wear the T-shirt, but Pauline had one on.

"Happy, happy!" Marika said to the writers. "Keep smiling! Whoever signs the most new members gets a prize!"

Suzanne dug her pen into the table, scratching out a groove as best she could on the plastic laminate.

"I didn't know we could win a prize," said Pauline.

"Yeah, probably a T-shirt or some other crap," said Gordon.

A sullen boy stood in front of Suzanne, who kept marking the table with ink.

"Your logo is stupid," he said.

"I know," she answered, not looking up.

"Why is your logo so stupid?"

"I don't know."

"My mum makes better logos on our computer."

"I know."

The kid grunted and trudged away.

"What time is it?" Suzanne asked.

"About twelve," said Gordon.

"That's it? We've only been here an hour? Do we have to stay until eight tonight? Who in their right mind would come tonight? It's going down to minus 35."

Gordon stretched his legs out under the table. "Yeah."

Suzanne rolled her shoulders a few times. She knew her attitude brought Gordon and Pauline down. She didn't like the idea of being a crank. A band of pain grew behind her eyes. She had to remind herself of her vow to change, to be the lamp on the nightstand instead of under the bushel. The sign in the open field she passed on the way to work spelled it out simply: Prepare To

Meet They God. Did Brady see the sign on his way to work? Did it mean anything to him? Did it prompt him to consider his ruinous management? Did it mean anything to her except rural superstition? She rubbed her eyes. Gothic kitsch. She massaged her temples.

"There's pizza and beer in John's office. Part of his 'Team ABS' kick. Better than nothing, I suppose," said Gordon.

"Oh yeah?" Suzanne perked up.

A young couple wearing parkas hovered around their table, glancing at the membership forms. Pauline smiled at them.

"Hi there. Membership in ABS starts as low as five dollars a month. You can donate in one lump sum or in monthly installments."

"Where does the money go?" asked the man.

"It all goes toward programming."

The young couple looked over the brochures. The woman handled a *This Day in Alberta* mug.

"That's a premium. If you pledge 120 dollars, or ten dollars a month, you receive the mug as a bonus," Pauline said.

"That's a lot to pay for a mug," said the man, smiling.

Suzanne focused on the man. A demonic energy asserted itself. Violence coursed through her veins.

"It'll be a lot more to pay later. I'm assuming you're together."

The young couple smiled at her. "Yes."

"Do you have any kids?"

"We have a two-year-old, Courtney. Courtney likes Rooey."

"Isn't that nice." Suzanne smiled back. She stood and clasped her hands. "Do yourselves a favour and support ABS right now. Because if ABS disappears and commercial-free television is gone from the airwaves, Courtney's going to grow up watching programming that will turn her into an automaton. Unless that's what you want, a compliant individual who will never think for herself."

"Himself," the woman said.

"Look. Some people want their children to be factory-issue, children who want nothing more than the latest consumer goods. Maybe you're these people, I don't know."

"No. We're not," said the man.

"Okay. Supporting commercial-free educational television is a way to protect your child from the nefarious forces of mainstream media. I guarantee if he watches nothing but ABS in his formative years, you'll never have to worry about him becoming greedy. No commercials means no promotion of artificial need, which, in the long run, will save you money."

The young couple looked at each other and nodded. "I guess."

"I bet that mug looks like a steal now for ten bucks a month." Sweat trickled down Suzanne's armpits. She turned a membership form around and eased it toward the couple. "Please support ABS. Do it for your family. Do it for Courtney. For his safety."

The man reached for his wife's hand. She looked at him and nodded. He picked up a pen and filled out the membership form.

"Thank you," he said, "thanks for talking to us."

"That's okay. Thanks for your support. God bless."

The young couple walked away, faces radiant with goodness. Suzanne sat down and folded her arms to hide trembling hands. Gordon and Pauline looked amazed.

"Where did that come from?" said Gordon.

"I don't know."

"Nefarious?"

"It is."

"Wow. Way to go. That was something else," said Pauline.

Suzanne resumed whittling away at the table with a pen. The exertion had left her unsettled. She wiped cold sweat from her forehead.

"Wait. Hold on. One, two, three," she said, pointing at Gordon, Pauline and herself. "Hey! Where's Leslie?"

"He's Rooey," said Pauline.

"What do you mean 'He's Rooey'?"

"Yeah, can you believe that? He volunteered and made a big deal about taking over. The regular Rooey's sick. Suck-ass," Gordon said, picking up a pen and drawing a smiley face on the back of an ABS pledge form.

"He's *Rooey*? Pauline, doesn't that gall you?"

"Why should it?"

"Because you invented Rooey. You *made* Rooey."

"I didn't invent him. I only made a suggestion about his hair. Then my suggestion was reviewed by a committee. Then another committee implemented his tuft of hair."

"Why does Leslie get to be Rooey? Why isn't he here, flogging memberships?"

"Because no one else wanted to put on that mangy suit," said Gordon.

Suzanne's mood curdled. She sneered and stared at the floor. She had no love for Rooey, but the thought of Leslie masquerading as the ABS ambassador and ingratiating himself to John Brady galled. The little children didn't know what menace lurked beneath. She fumed at the image of happy children hugging Leslie. His opportunism besmirched Rooey. She'd expose him as an imposter, for the sake of the children. She grabbed her coat.

"I'm going to get some pizza. Hold the fort."

Suzanne navigated her way through knots of families touring the cubicles and photocopying machines. She entered John's office, the predictable corner suite, and helped herself to a beer from a case. She guzzled half and held the bottle in her coat pocket. She jogged down the stairs to the basement and the studios. A few ABS technicians manned the control rooms, making sure no one touched the consoles. Suzanne stuck her head in. Parents and children gazed at the rows of television monitors on the wall, each specific to a studio camera or VTR playback machine. The marvel she felt at seeing a television control room, a genuinely impressive technological nerve centre, never waned. She understood the general public's awe.

"Hey, Pete, is Rooey down here?"

"Yeah, he's in Studio A."

She headed down a brightly lit corridor and eased her way by a knot of people outside the makeup room. She stood on tiptoes to see the attraction. She glimpsed Jason in a makeup chair, wearing a bib and having powder applied to his visage. He addressed the crowd.

"Makeup is necessary on television because it evens out the skin tone. This is a special kind of makeup, not the sort of thing you'd wear out on the street, unless you were looking for a good time, if you know what I mean."

A few people laughed reluctantly at his joke. Suzanne sighed.

She continued down the hallway, past clusters of adults, and into Studio A. Lit by a couple of spots on the studio grid, the *This Day in Alberta* set was overrun with gleeful toddlers and loafing teenagers. Off to the side, Rooey stood flapping his flipper limbs, his giant head bobbing on his disproportionate body. Children swarmed in a semicircle around him, waiting their turn to receive a hug. Rooey's manic eyes and deranged grin didn't upset or frighten them.

Suzanne hid behind a heavy studio curtain. What could she do but watch? To rip off the mascot head would surely cost her the membership gig. Apparently, seeing the person underneath the costume caused great trauma for kids. Even she thought the deed too extreme. She sucked back the remainder of the beer and glowered.

However. A swift kick to the balls was surely okay in the mascot harassment playbook. The children wouldn't be horrified if their beloved pal buckled over and dropped to the floor. They'd think it was a game.

From the shadows of the curtains came two voices, young teenaged boys stifling laughter.

"Fuckin' fuck!"

"Rooey's like a big freak!"

Suzanne brightened. She saw them idling on a storage bin against the wall. Teenagers could always be counted on not to understand the consequences of their actions. She walked toward them, smelling the pot on their clothes.

"Excuse me," she said, "but I couldn't help overhearing your conversation."

The two teens slid off the storage bin and slouched, hair over their faces. "What conversation?"

She dug in her pocket and produced five dollars. "Wanna get high?"

"Sure!" they said.

"Then do me this. Go kick Rooey in the crotch. Then get the hell out." She waved the bill. "Here, I trust you. You look like honest types."

"Cool!" The youth with the tattoo on his neck plucked the bill from her hand.

She emerged from the darkness. An ABS volunteer wiped up a large spill on one of the *This Day in Alberta* chairs while a cross parent scolded a crying toddler. Rooey continued to delight the children, flapping his tiny limbs. Certain that Leslie hadn't spotted her, Suzanne headed to the exit and leaned in the Studio A door frame.

"Ooooo, roooo!" sang Rooey.

Suddenly from the curtains, the laughing teens charged. In the bright light of the studio, teen number one wound up and kicked Rooey in the furry groin, followed immediately by teen number two planting his knee in between Rooey's legs.

"OOOOOOO, ROOOOOO!!!"

Rooey crumpled to the floor. The whooping teens rushed out of the studio. The group of children who gathered around Rooey showed no distress at seeing their buddy buckled over and writhing. Instead, they laughed uproariously. One raucous preschooler took a swing at Rooey's crotch. Other crazed preschoolers joined in, kicking Rooey in the ribs, crotch and the head. Rooey dragged himself away from the attack.

"OOOOOO, ROOOOOOOOOOOO!!!"

Suzanne grinned. She knew the character of Rooey couldn't say anything other than "Ooooo, Roooo." Leslie wouldn't break down and scream "Fuck off." That would incur penalty.

An ABS volunteer noticed the rumble. "Good lord!"

Another ABS volunteer, hawking raffle tickets, heeded the commotion. "Oh my God, stop it! Stop kicking Rooey!"

Content, Suzanne slipped away to shouts of "Stop it!" and "Rooey needs first aid!"

Outside the makeup room Jason stood, bib on and foundation caking his face, watching people scurry away. "What's going on?"

"I don't know. I'm just trying to find the washroom."

"Why aren't people paying attention to me any more?"

Feeling cocky, Suzanne let herself into Jason's dressing room and shut the door. "I'll pay attention to you. Can I use your toilet?"

Jason looked at Suzanne. She shuffled from foot to foot, grinning. She felt his quick scan of her narrow jaw, thinning eyebrows and glazed blue eyes hinting derangement. She wanted to tell him to fuck off. He put his hands on his hips and thrust out his jaw.

"Yes. Yeah. You can use my toilet."

Suzanne stopped grinning. She shoved her hands in her pockets and stiffened. She took in his highlighted blond hair, broad cheekbones and narrow eyes. She caught a vibe. Neglect. She knew it.

"Thanks."

She struggled to piss knowing he was close.

In an employee lounge, Suzanne and Gordon eavesdropped as feeding ABS employees chatted about the Rooey incident.

"Who's the guy?"

"Leslie, one of the pledge writers."

"Is he okay?"

"Yeah, but Rooey's out of commission for the rest of the day. We told the kids Rooey had to go back to the Land of Oooooroooo. A few cried, but most of them were still giddy."

"Apparently two guys started it."

"I guess. We'll probably never know."

Suzanne tapped her beer bottle with Gordon's pop can. Her eyelids heavy, she smiled. The couple of Ativan she'd washed down with beer slowed her. She sank into the couch beside Gordon. She grinned inanely and raised the beer bottle to her lips. Any more alcohol and she'd have trouble walking.

"I hate to say it, but Leslie being mugged by kids, I wish I had seen it," said Gordon

"It was brilliant."

"Suzanne, did you still want to get together about membership?"

Her gut tightened. She leaned forward and put the beer down carefully, staring at her shoes. "We could do that."

"What about this Thursday? Where should we meet?"

"I dunno. Where do you should we meet, think we meet?"

Gordon nudged her leg. "Are you okay?"

She lifted her head, smiled and leaned back. Her eyes felt like slits. "Never better. This is the year of living!"

"We should get back. Pauline is probably wondering where we are. She's probably still sitting there."

Suzanne babbled, the words bouncing like a rubber ball.

"Let's go Teddy's. On Jasper. By me place. Iz okay? Food's good. Round seven?"

Gordon lifted from the couch. He wrapped two slices of pizza in tin foil. "Yeah, that sounds like a plan. I'll just clear it with Ryan's mom. It should be fine, though."

Aloft in a gossamer intoxication, she could only manage a weak response to the spectre of Ryan's mom. She heaved herself from the couch and stumbled into an ABS administrative assistant.

"Whoops. Sorry, man. Are you okay?"

"Are *you* okay?" asked the woman.

Back at the membership table, Pauline listened to the complaints of a member. He sported a bow tie, an admirable touch in minus-30-degree weather.

"But really, why doesn't Bernard McPhail visit Alberta? He has many fans here. I think it rather an affront," said the red-headed man.

"I understand how you must feel, sir."

"Well then. Do something about it."

"I assure you I will take your concerns to our Audience Relations Department."

Gordon and Suzanne took their seats behind the table. The red-headed man addressed them.

"Are you with Audience Relations?"

"No," said Gordon.

"I am," slurred Suzanne, standing up and leaning on the table.

Pauline glared at Suzanne and then at Gordon. Gordon shook his head.

The red-headed man regarded Suzanne. "Yes, well, I was just explaining to this woman that I'd like to see Bernard McPhail visit Alberta sometime. It doesn't have to be Edmonton, my wife and I would be willing to drive to Calgary."

Bernard McPhail was the actor who played Inspector Hawthorne. Suzanne burped into her sweater.

"He has many fans here in Alberta. I've been a loyal supporter of ABS for over fifteen years. Surely we could arrange some sort of celebration for Inspector Hawthorne."

Suzanne scratched her neck. "Okay, sir, first of all the *Inspector Hawthorne* series is twenty years old. They haven't made any new ones since then, haven't even made a Movie of the Week. Second, Bernard McPhail, I believe, is ill with colon cancer, but you would know that because you're a fan. And third, ABS doesn't have enough money to pay its contract workers, let alone the cost of trips for British actors to have tea with viewers. The way to celebrate the programming you love is to maintain your ABS membership. Have you renewed your membership yet?"

The red-headed man cleared his throat. "Well, no, as a matter of fact."

Suzanne pushed a membership form and a pen toward him.

"Don't you think that your continued financial support is vital to our survival? You want to safeguard quality television. I know you do. You're an intelligent man. I can see that. Make a commitment to programming like *Inspector Hawthorne*, right now. Just write down your credit card number and the amount you'd like to donate and we'll take care of the rest. Do it for Bernard McPhail, who for all we know is languishing in a hospital bed somewhere in England."

The red-headed man appeared to ponder her words. He searched his breast pocket and pulled out an elegant pen. "I have my own pen, madam. Thank you for the reminder to renew. I appreciate your candour." He filled out a form, bowed and strode away.

Gordon stared at Suzanne and shook his head.

"I don't get it. Do you love this place or hate it?"

Pauline leaned back in her chair, her anger at their late return defused. "You're good, Suzanne."

Suzanne peered around the landing. Suddenly she had sobered up, as if some hawk had clutched her from the Land of Oooooroooo and dropped her in an exam. The effects of beer and Ativan had evaporated too quickly. It was the dreaded scourge of membership, she realized, the hard-wiring of practised argument. She thudded back in her chair before another member of the public needing information. She buried her head in her hands, feeling unaccountable shame.

Gordon excused himself to go to the washroom, leaving Pauline and Suzanne alone. Pauline fidgeted with a mug. Without knitting needles, she seemed lost.

"Suzanne. Suzanne."

Suzanne lifted her head. Pauline shifted over to Gordon's chair. She spoke softly. "I, uh, think we should discuss this membership business you wanted to talk about. Remember? Something about writing bad membership scripts so Jason looks like an idiot?"

Brooding, Suzanne flared her nostrils at the recollection of the treasonous plot. "Right."

"Have you talked to Gordon about it?"

"Yeah, we're meeting this week to talk. He's interested."

"What about Leslie?"

"Forget Leslie, especially today."

"Why don't I talk to him?"

"If you think it would help, sure."

Pauline fiddled with a membership form. "I haven't signed up anyone yet. You've done two."

"I'm lucky, that's all."

"No. You have the gift of the gab."

Gab. So that was what infested her mind, kept her staring at the ceiling at night, haunting her dreams. Gab.

"Pauline, do you ever feel elated one minute and despair the next?"

Pauline pursed her lips. "Can't say that I do."

Suzanne looked at her. "That's where gab comes from."

Back from the washroom, Gordon stopped in front of the announcements posted by the elevator. He seemed unable to walk by a flyer without reading it. Suzanne glanced at Pauline's wristwatch. Another five hours of being in this particular public. She would need fortification.

"I'll be back," she said, pulling on her coat.

Lathering her hands and gazing at the reflections in the mirror, Suzanne emitted gas. She listened to a mother speaking with her two children.

"Emma. Yes, we'll go after this. Emma. Hurry up. It doesn't flush? Don't worry. Kayla, have you washed your hands? Yes, Mummy washed her hands. We have to wash our hands every time we go to the bathroom, right? Emma, wash your hands. We're going to see Oma after this. Do you want some snacks? We'll have snacks in the car."

Emma let the water run. On tiptoes she reached for the soap dispenser and pumped a dollop. Carefully, studiously, she washed her little hands. Suzanne caught Emma in the mirror looking at her. Suzanne wiped her hands with a paper towel and tossed it toward the garbage. Thinking how small children were, how little their hands and bodies, and how they can't fight back, she floated into a stall and shut the door.

She guessed Emma's age to be six. In four years she would be Diana's age, and could smoke cigarettes and let an old man take pictures of her and a blond boy doing things naked. She could make some money to feed her little sister.

Suzanne rolled the vial of Ativan in her hand. A couple more would help her relax. A couple more pills would help her exist in this world, and help her forget the other world behind her eyes where tectonic plates were about to shift.

The cold clawed her. Cheeks and nose and mouth stung. Staggering onward, stumbling into snow, falling. The black sky like hockey tape, taut and worn. Wobbling up and one foot in front of the other, weaving to a bus shelter. Only fifteen feet away. Only ten feet away. Tripping and falling on the sidewalk, on her knees. Crawling to the shelter and struggling to stand. Crashing onto a hard plastic bench and hitting her head on the Plexiglas.

Distant light glimmered. Warehouses and offices lined the empty white street, dark structures housing products and numbers and industry. This bus shelter, a square box among the other square boxes, temporary sanctuary. Her ears rang.

"Shit."

She pulled her toque down and clasped the edges to her chin. Mouth dry and numb, she ran her tongue over her teeth and lips. She wasn't unconscious, or subconscious, but paleo-conscious, her core an icy, uninhabitable pole. Wind-swept nothingness, absolute zero. The last circle of hell.

"Where's the fuckin' bus?"

Her toes stung. She covered her face with her gloves and breathed. Gusts shook the Plexiglas. She curled her fingers in her gloves to keep the tips warm. The shelter levelled out in her vision. A bus shelter. In the middle of nowhere, in the middle of winter, in Edmonton, Alberta. She hugged herself and buried her face in her coat. Rooey. She smiled. Rooey had his ass kicked. Why did his assault make her happy? She shook with cold. He never hurt anyone. Rooey loved kids. Gentle, sweet Rooey. Rooey was like her young lover, Colin. Lovely, trusting Colin. Attack Rooey and you attack Colin, and she would never do that. Innocent children and mascots needed protection. What had she done? She had corrupted him. Colin and Rooey.

She hoisted herself up on jelly legs. She shuffled from side to side, trying to keep warm. Tears welled and streamed down her cheeks. She screwed her face and sobbed, pressing her head against the Plexiglas. Her knees buckled and she fell to the ground. She knelt and wiped strings of mucus from her nose and mouth.

She sensed light and raised her head. Two distant glows came closer. She crawled from the shelter and reached out to the light that was becoming larger and brighter in the blackness.

She mewed, an injured, sick animal.

"I almost made Employee of the Month. Came really close. I worked lots of overtime, and a few customers commented on my helpfulness. I find being of assistance works. They like that. It's that simple. Maybe next month. What are you looking for again?"

"Ibuprofen."

"Want me to ask that customer service rep over there?"

"No."

"Okay, Pumpkin."

Colin followed behind her like an obedient dog. She knew exactly where the analgesics were, what aisle, what shelves. She'd buy them in bulk if they offered club packs. A stronger anti-inflammatory might calm the swelling, but without a prescription, extra-strength generic painkillers had to suffice. They bought the ibuprofen and crossed the street to her apartment. The night sky, a black pool, drew her in. Sharp pain stabbed behind one eye.

The Fellow stirred as she opened the vestibule door. She fished for her keys. Wide-eyed, Colin watched the Fellow with fascination.

"Don't worry about him," she said. "He comes by every now and then."

Without saying anything, Colin clung to Suzanne's coat. He peeked at the Fellow from over her shoulder. She checked her mailbox. A phone bill and a notice from Canadian Blood Services, inviting her to a blood drive in two weeks. She didn't mind giving blood, rather liked it. She enjoyed the sensation of a needle digging deep in her arm. She hoped that by siphoning off a pint of sludge she'd generate new, vibrant blood. Clean blood. She still banked on her body having the capacity to renew itself.

"Everything's all right," said the Fellow, grinning at a conversation going on in his head. "It's all right."

Suddenly her stomach heaved and boiled. Forcing down a surge of vileness, she rested her forehead against the mailboxes.

"Have everything?" asked Colin.

"Uh, yeah." She rubbed her eyes and unlocked the door to the apartments. Sweat trickled down her armpits. She stopped.

"Mr. Fellow, I want to let you in. But I can't. I'm not allowed. Stay here for a while, it's not too cold. I'm sorry. There's always the homeless shelter down the street." She looked at him sorrowfully. He chuckled a bit but then his expression changed, like a cloud had passed over him. His face drooped and his head bobbed.

They climbed the wide staircase, radiators tapping and hissing. Wilma was heading downstairs, taking each step with care.

"Well, hello!"

Suzanne hadn't seen Wilma lately. Wilma's face was wan and her coat hung loosely. She had lost some weight. Cancer seemed to agree with her.

"Look who it is. My long-lost neighbour. The neighbour who never calls or knocks on my door."

"Hi. How are you?"

"Still alive. And I see you have a little friend."

Suzanne had so far successfully smuggled Colin in and out of the building without detection. She didn't want to hear Wilma make awkward comments, like the one she made now. Suzanne didn't want to justify her relationship with a fresh-faced young man barely out of high school.

"I'm Suzanne's boyfriend, Colin," he said, extending his hand. "How do you do?"

Wilma shook his hand and nodded at Suzanne. "Well, well, well. Boyfriend, eh? So that's what all that noise is I hear coming from your place. That's what that muffled pounding is. Now I get it."

Suzanne winced. "How are you feeling?"

"Lousy. I started chemo. It's like Drano. Hey—that rhymes."

"Why don't we talk later," Suzanne said, continuing up the stairs.

"Yes. Why don't we?"

"Nice to meet you," said Colin, following Suzanne to her door.

"And very nice to meet you," Wilma said in a singsong voice, turning to watch them. As Suzanne let herself and Colin in the apartment, she heard Wilma whistle.

"She seemed nice," said Colin.

Suzanne tore into the ibuprofen and downed three pills. Her head still throbbed from two nights ago. The day after the ABS Open House, she'd woken up fully dressed on her bed. Staggering to the toilet to cough up mucus and blood, shaking and weak, she looked at herself in the mirror. A rash lined her swollen blue eyes and splotchy cheeks. New blood vessels had found their way to her skin's surface. Blond and grey hair matted on one side of her head. Her uneven lips sagged at the corners. Her brain thrashed against her skull, beating with excruciating pain. She had stumbled back to bed and remained there until three hours ago.

Visual snippets before she blacked out: snow, hands and arms lifting her, a car, low and dark.

Colin pulled off his boots, removed his mitts and coat, and continued to undress. She leaned in the kitchen door frame and watched. He stepped out of his pants and pulled his T-shirt and sweater over his head. He sat on the edge of the bed and peeled off his socks. He stood and stripped off his underwear. In less than a minute he was naked, skin pink, penis erect. He slid under the duvet.

This had been their routine for a few weeks, Colin coming over to the apartment for lovemaking sessions. Sometimes tender but often torrid, they sank into each other for hours. Colin had mastered sex quickly, his callowness vanishing. Unsure, afraid, she pondered the body under the covers. He propped himself up on a pillow and ran his hand over the duvet cover.

"What's the matter? Come on."

She sighed and turned the light out in the kitchen. Six hours ago she'd wished she were dead.

"Okay. Lemme see if I have any messages first."

She sat by the phone, kicked off her boots and pressed a button on the answering machine. One message.

"Hi, Suzanne, this is Marika at ABS. Suzanne, could you please give me a call as soon as you get this message? Thanks."

A fantastic effervescence spread through her limbs. The darkness sizzled in her ears.

"Colin, I'm not feeling too well."

"Aw. Poor baby. Come on. Come under the covers."

Panic made her heart ratchet up. In her mind she was in a cartoon running against a recurring background. Table, lamp, chair. Table, lamp, chair. Someone dribbling her head. Boing. Sprong. Zoicks! She crawled into bed, clothes still on.

"Okay, Colin, this is what we're going to do. I'm going to lie still and breathe. You're going to get up and get me a drink of water."

He ran the kitchen tap while Suzanne rested her hand on her heart. A few deep breaths and the cartoon horror would go away. A weasel clobbered her with a hammer. Splang!

Colin handed her the water. She searched for some Ativan, security like a nightlight.

"Are you okay now?"

She took two pills. "I will be."

He drew her close to him, caressing her arm. "There, there."

Snuggling into his chest, she tried to hide from the weasel. It all came down to the basic riddle: *What have I done?* Marika had never called her at home before. She wanted her to call the office ASAP. Why? *What have I done?* The last thing Suzanne recalled about the Open House was putting her arm around an elderly woman and howling "Ooooo, Roooo!"

"Ah, Colin, remember I told you I had to work the ABS Open House?"

"Yeah. I wanted to go. I wanted to see Rooey but you wouldn't let me."

"Yeah. Well. I can't remember what I did there."

He kissed her head and cuddled her. "You silly."

"You know, maybe, maybe I shouldn't drink as much as I do. Give it a rest for now. It's making me sick."

"Well, if that's what you want to do, I support you."

"Why don't you drink?"

"I don't like it."

She nestled her head under his chin. Colin once again astonished her with his sweetness. She wished she could see through his eyes, to see life as clearly and simply as he did. Alcohol he didn't like. Sexual intercourse he did like. Mindless self-destruction he didn't like. Stacking new products at the Home Depot he did like. She could learn a lot from Colin.

"Look," he said, unzipping her fleece pullover, "there's not much you can do about what happened, or didn't happen." He blew into her hands to warm them. "We're here now, safe and sound. No one can get us."

He's right, she thought. Whatever debacle occurred at the Open House was history. She'd have to face Marika's condescension and John's disciplinary action. What's done is done. She'd been through the remorse shtick before, she'd survive it now. Colin's words calmed her. The cartoon world faded. She sat up and removed her T-shirt, bra and jeans. She snuggled into his chest and hugged him.

"Oh, Colin. Why do I do these things?"

He cupped her chin and stroked her cheek. "Why do any of us do anything?"

"You're so wise."

"No, I'm not. It's like what my camp counsellors used to say—time out, slow down, sit still."

"Stop, look and listen."

"That as well."

He pulled her to him. They kissed softly. He caressed her ass, tugging her underwear. Soothed, she slid on top of him. She wiggled a bit, but stopped.

"You went to camp? I never went to camp."

"Yeah. It was fun. I made friends."

"Do you ever see these friends?"

"No. They had to go to a different school." He touched her breasts and tweaked her nipples. She stalled.

"What do you mean, 'a different school'?"

"They went to another school. The camp was for kids with special needs from across Edmonton, not just my area." He drew her breasts to his mouth.

She squeezed her eyes shut. From sepia ground they popped; mice with huge ears and vicious buckteeth. They squeaked and giggled, darted and dashed until they charged, the mind mice brigade, each one with a hammer. Bam! Pow! Spluggada, spluggada, spluggada until the lights went out.

CHAPTER 16—DAMAGE CONTROL

"You're fucking a retard?!" cried Jackie.

"Don't say that."

"You just said, 'I'm fucking a retard.'"

"I didn't say that. I said I'm fucking someone with a possible developmental disability. *You* said he was a retard!"

"What does a developmental disability mean?"

"I don't know. I'm not sure."

"Does he have Down Syndrome?"

"No, he doesn't have Down Syndrome! Come on! Not to say people with Down Syndrome aren't cute."

"Is he uncoordinated?"

"I'm uncoordinated, for Christ's sake!"

"Well then, how is he developmentally disabled?"

"He went to a special camp."

"So? We hung out with people who went to a special camp."

"That's juvie hall, that's a different kind of special."

"Why are you fucking a twenty-year-old in the first place? Look, I'm the last person in the world who wants to be judgmental, but—"

"But what? Come on, don't do this to me. I don't need a lecture right now, I need support."

"Support for what? Fucking a retard?"

"I AM NOT FUCKING A RETARD!"

Suzanne scowled short rapid puffs into the receiver. She listened to the clear telephone line, no buzz, no static to blame the silence on. They edged toward confrontation.

"All I thought," Suzanne said quietly, "was that you'd, I don't know, laugh, or have some compassion for me."

"I do. But . . ." Jackie's voice trailed.

Suzanne gripped the receiver and stared hard at the floor. While their conversations the last few times had been as animated as usual, a soft melancholy had tinged them. Belief in each other's infallibility was subsiding. Suzanne felt ten years old, hopelessly clinging to the illusion of Santa Claus. The alternative, the flat unknown, was too onerous.

"I don't know what to say, Suz. I'm sorry you found out he's not, well, that he's slow. But at least now, when people ask, you can say you're seeing someone special."

Suzanne laughed. "There you go! That's what I need, you making fun of me. Hack on me, take your best shots. I'm an idiot."

"What are you going to do?"

"The honourable thing, break it off. Too bad, though. He doesn't seem slow to me."

"Maybe you're slow."

"No, that's not it. He's just very good-natured. What's wrong with that? Maybe he went to the special camp for being exceedingly sweet. Since when has that become a disability?"

"Ever think that this so-called special camp was just a dumping ground for kids whose parents had the real problems?"

"You're right. So you're saying I should still fuck him."

"No. But maybe he's not as developmentally disabled as you think. No slanted eyes, no problems with motor skills."

"*Nyet.*"

"Well," said Jackie, "don't jump to conclusions. Forgive yourself and move on. Let him go."

Suzanne sipped water and felt uplifted by Jackie's absolution. Jackie. So kind. So selfless. So much like her.

"Thanks, Johnson. Hey, are you working on a painting?"

"No. No time."

"You have to! I get headaches when you don't paint."

"Don't worry."

"That's the hollow advice I give my neighbour."

"Listen," said Jackie. "Why don't you do something to get your mind off your fascinating yet tiresome self? We've been doing this for a while and you might find it, I dunno, nice. It's just a suggestion. Martin and I have sponsored a foster child for the last few months."

Suzanne tightened her hold on the water glass. "A foster child? What do you mean? A kid lives with you? Do you get paid for this?"

"No, the kid does not live with us. We sponsor a child in Africa. We're doing it through Foster Plan for Kids. They take the money out of your bank account every month and it goes toward the kid."

"You're shilling for Foster Kids now? Put that money toward public broadcasting!"

"It might be nice for you to care for a kid. You get pictures of the kid, and the kid receives your financial support."

"I already give to ABS."

"Cut down on ABS and give to a foster child. Come on, what happened to the new you? Who knows—maybe the kids in Africa get *Rooey's Playschool Adventures* on TV."

Suzanne grimaced. "This is what is known as peer pressure."

"It's just a suggestion."

"Why are you doing this?"

Jackie cleared her throat. "I don't know. Wanting to make it better for kids, this time around."

Suzanne nodded into the receiver. Making it better, this time around. For who? Nobody gave a fuck. Nobody made it better for her except Mr. Audi, who made her feel sick. Audi: his balding head, his thick glasses, his button-down shirts. His dusty apartment where the kids met him. *Show me yours. Here's a ten.* Diana could buy some candy now, choke it down, and bring some home for her little sister. Jackie would be waiting in a booth nearby at the Silver Moon restaurant, not knowing where her best friend had been. Suzanne would arrive jumpy, smiling, and ready to order pizza with Jackie, her anchor, her safe harbour, her audience.

"All right. I'll look into it."

"Good!"

Suzanne closed her eyes. *Come on, Santa. Come on, Santa. Don't go, Santa. Don't go. You bastard.*

CHAPTER 17—MANOEUVRE #3

Toast of New York. She smoothed on the lipstick, the thin film of mauve moistening her lips. Would this make her the toast of Edmonton? Jasper Avenue? She'd bought the lipstick because of the name, buckling to faint hope. She examined herself in her bathroom mirror. The rash had almost cleared up, and under-eye concealer made the red dots less noticeable. Freshly washed and combed hair framed her face. She smiled. Lipstick lined her front teeth. She wiped it away and blotted her lips. She made a face in the mirror and left.

Teddy's glowed with welcome. She entered the restaurant, the smell of bacon grease and French fries warming the air. Gordon sat at a booth on the upper level. He wore a fleece pullover with a "Jasper National Park" logo. Suzanne waved at him and kept waving until she stood at the booth. She felt high at the sight of her secret crush. Something about him seemed trustworthy.

"I'm here!" she beamed.

He smiled.

She slid onto the bench across from him. She looked at his hands, wide, big, masculine.

"So."

"So," he said.

She forgot the reason they were there. It now seemed like pretense.

"Have you been waiting long?"

"No. About ten minutes. Didn't you say you lived across the street?"

"Yeah. I had to, uh—"

"Come on, you just wanted to be fashionably late, like at the ABS meetings!"

She smiled at his teasing. Ostensibly, they were there to discuss a strategy for dealing with John and Jason and the phasing out of their jobs. Her job. She hadn't phoned Marika back. Marika had called again, leaving another message saying they needed to hear from her urgently. Terror and quivering sickness had stopped her from returning the call. She knew she was done. The writing job she'd cursed for three years now abruptly and heartlessly gone, without pity for her weak and sensitive soul.

Suzanne looked around for a waiter. "Wanna beer?"

"No thanks. You were quite the handful the other night."

"I was? When?"

"At the Open House. How much did you have to drink, anyway?"

Suzanne rubbed her eyes and then stopped, remembering she had mascara on. "Oh, that."

"I used to drink that way when I was camping. Fell in a fire once. I don't do that any more."

"Do what?"

"Get drunk. Or drink, for that matter."

Suzanne eyed him. Was he some kind of reformer?

"Yeah, I don't know. Guess I overdid it. Hope no one is pissed at me."

"Marika could have killed you. I think people thought you were playing a character, until they realized that you were actually drunk."

"Did I do anything?"

"You don't remember pretending you were interviewing people for *This Day in Alberta*?"

"Yeesh."

"I covered for you—told people it was your fortieth birthday. A milestone."

"Oh, it might be a milestone, all right."

"Then you just disappeared. At around five or so. You scared Pauline."

"Did I look drunk?"

"You were still on your feet. Then."

A waiter came by to take their orders.

"Brady's out to destroy us, you know," she said, changing the subject. "Try the Reuben, it's great. It sits in your gut for days soaking up transgressions."

"So it's Brady who's out to destroy us," he said, smiling a bit.

Gordon radiated health. What kind of a human being didn't drink? Odd.

"Yes," she said. "You know it and I know it. We would be remiss if we allowed Brady and his ilk to annihilate educational public television in Alberta, if not the country. What's next, the CBC? No. No, I say!" She slammed her fist on the table.

Gordon laughed. "Come on."

Suzanne grinned at her own theatrics. "Okay, but. But. But what I proposed to Pauline is that we write awful membership scripts, full of nonsense, to discredit Jason. I guarantee he doesn't know fact from fiction."

"Ah. A conspiracy. I like it. What did she say?"

"She's on board."

"What about Leslie?"

"She said she'd talk to him. Look, we're all going to be sacked anyway after this. And one of us staying on is probably a lie. Let's get Lawrence his old job back."

Gordon smiled again. "You're serious."

"Absolutely. We have nothing to lose."

"Why does any of this matter to you so much?"

Suzanne looked out the window for inspiration, but caught her reflection instead. "I have to care about something."

Gordon leaned back and clasped his hands on top of his head. "Well. I think these guys are pompous fools. And I am going to start up my bike store—"

"Bike store?"

"—and I do like and respect Lawrence and Frank." He looked back at Suzanne and grinned. "Yeah, why not?"

Their food arrived. Suzanne raised her Reuben in a toast. "To the defeat of the infidel."

Gordon smiled. "To the defeat of the infidel." Their sandwiches touched. "I helped you, in case you're wondering. It was me. I understand."

She salted her sandwich. "Helped me? When did I need help?"

"The other night. At the bus shelter."

She squeezed her sandwich, her fingertips making an imprint in the bread. "So, Ryan seems like a nice kid."

Gordon glanced over her head. "Hey. Is that Jason? Over there, by the door?"

She whipped around. A head of blond streaks and a low brow acknowledged them. He smiled and sauntered toward their table. He wore a tan cashmere coat.

"Pretend you don't see him," she said.

"Hi, Jason."

Jason smiled and shook hands with Gordon, then pumped Suzanne's hand. "Mind if I join you?"

"Truthfully, we were having a quiet—"

"Sure. Have a seat," said Gordon.

Suzanne sulked, the tantalizing possibilities of the evening yanked away by a miscreant.

Jason slid in beside her. "I hope I'm not interrupting anything. Are you two an item? What happened to the kid at the mall?"

"What kid at the mall?" asked Gordon.

"NOTHING," said Suzanne.

Jason caught the waiter's attention. "Do you have a wine list?"

The waiter stifled a laugh and indicated the menu card behind the ketchup. Jason looked over the offerings and ordered a beer. "So, what's happening?"

"What's happening?" said Suzanne.

"Yeah. What's happening? What does one do in Edmonton? Where are the hip spots in town? Is this one? Maybe with the types who think this place is so uncool it's cool."

Under the table, Suzanne kicked Gordon.

"I bring my son here sometimes. He's seven," said Gordon.

Jason drummed his fingers on the table. "Do you mind if I sit next to you, Gordon? I want to be able to see what's going on. I'm just facing you and a brick wall right now."

Jason swivelled over to Gordon's side of the booth. Suzanne made no attempt to disguise her sour expression. Jason's beer arrived.

"So Suzanne, you're from Toronto, right?"

"God, no."

"I thought you were."

"I lived in Toronto. I was never *from* Toronto."

"I'm from Toronto," Jason said. "Canada hates Toronto. Know why? People are ignorant. And jealous. What a stupid national pastime."

"Why are you in Edmonton?" asked Gordon.

"Good one!" said Jason, raising his glass.

"Yeah, why *are* you in Edmonton?" said Suzanne.

"I go where the opportunity is. John hand-picked me."

"Like some kind of vegetable," Suzanne muttered.

"I like Canada. I learn something every time I go somewhere." Jason gulped his beer. "I like ABS. Nice little place. I could learn a lot. What are you guys drinking? Let me buy you both a drink." Jason pulled a bill from his wallet and put it on the table. Gathering his gloves, he smiled. "Look, guys, I appreciate the writing you do for the membership campaigns. I really do. I can handle it from here on in, don't worry. If this really is your last campaign working at ABS, let's make it a great one. Where did you say the hip clubs were?"

"Try Whyte Avenue," said Gordon.

"I'll find them, don't worry. See you, guys."

He left. Gordon looked at Suzanne. "Did the guy we're giving the brush-off to just give us the brush-off?"

"I used to see it happen all the time," said Suzanne. "Why'd you let him sit down?"

"Just being polite. What were we talking about, before?"

"His imminent demise." She fingered the fiver Jason left. "Idiot. This isn't enough to buy drinks."

"I'm just glad I saw the front of the back I'm going to stab."

She slouched and looked over at the bar. Two men laughed with the bartender. An Oilers game swirled on TV. At the booth across from Suzanne and Gordon, a young couple lingered over coffee. She watched them smile shyly at each other. She wanted to ask Gordon about Ryan, about Ryan's mom. Her emotion stuck on Jason. She ran her tongue over her teeth.

"Marika phoned me," Suzanne blurted. "She wants me to phone her back. Gord. I'm worried. I think I'm being fired. The Open House and all."

"You don't know that for sure."

"Why else would she phone? Why her and not Frank?"

He dabbed some fries in ketchup. "Frank's pretty absent these days. I didn't see him once at Open House. Look. If you're fired, feel good that we're all toast. I'm sorry, Suzanne. I really am. And I'm sorry you got so drunk."

She gazed at him sadly. She could open up to him. He could be her Open House. Maybe he could love her.

"Why did you leave Toronto?" he asked.

She sighed. "You really want to know?"

"Try me."

She had a sip of beer and squinted at his intelligent eyes. "Okay. All right." She leaned forward, resting her elbows on the table. "I worked in master control at a TV station once. You know what master control is?"

He nodded. "Sure. Broadcast operations."

"Yeah. I faked my way into the job. So I'm on the midnight shift, because I can't deal with the daytime any more. One night I shut it off. All of it. I sat at the controls and faded everything to black. All the images—the cars, laughing people, toilet bowel cleaners, hair shampoos, fast food—gone. Disappeared. No broadcast. Security came for me. I waited for them. I just wanted peace. For everything to be still. Call it a protest."

Gordon leaned back and looked at her. "Why are you telling me this?"

"Like I said, at this point, what have we got to lose? What have I got to lose?"

CHAPTER 18—WHIPLASH

She sat upright in bed, drenched from a night of menacing dreams. An accountant she had outraged, a grocer she'd inadvertently insulted, a manicurist angry for no other reason than that she existed. Ugly pockmarked faces closing in on her, one mouth forward, incisors ready to shred.

She woke with a start, alone. After Teddy's, Gordon had walked Suzanne across the street and to the front door of her building. They'd agreed that they had both enjoyed their dinner together, exchanging shy smiles that suggested need. Gordon had bowed his head and wished her a good night. Now, slick and cold from nocturnal imaginings, she wondered if she should think about Gordon at all. What would he morph into?

There was a knock at the door. She slid under the duvet and held her breath, feeling Wilma's presence.

"I know you're in there. Answer the goddamn door!"

Avoiding her took extra resolve these days. Suzanne wrapped herself in the duvet and opened the door to Wilma, who wore a leopard-print coat and held a mass of red hair.

"Here it is! My crowning glory."

Suzanne flinched at Wilma's bald head and gawked at the wig Wilma brandished.

"That's a wig."

Wilma rubbed her head. "Just call me Kojak. *Who loves ya, baby?!* Haven't heard you banging your boy lately. What's going on?"

Suzanne eased the door closed. "Nice to see you. I have to get to work. Let's talk later. Congratulations on your purchase."

Wilma laughed and whistled as she went down the stairs.

There was no way around it. Suzanne would have to call Marika this morning. Three days had gone by since the phone call, each hour growing dimmer. She would also have to call Colin, who had phoned when she was out with Gordon. Call Colin, to end their sexual encounters and friendship. In the shower, she let the hot water turn her skin red. No more job, no more sex. She dried herself carelessly.

Tea mug in hand, wearing a sweatshirt and army pants, she pondered the phone. A rejection of this magnitude, of this finality, needed psychological readying. All the years of service to ABS gone: Lawrence reminding viewers to call the number on the screen; Cal Nagy and Katrina Demchuk, the hosts of *This Day in Alberta*, bantering awkwardly; Rooey, dear, grotesque Rooey. It had all nudged her toward mental disorder on many occasions, but she'd served ABS as a grateful steward. And now, these *people* with avarice in their eyes had overtaken the channel and banished the righteous. She wished to smite them. That's why she'd chosen to be inebriated beyond recognition at the Open House. To smite them. She had a sip of tea and stared into the mug. No curdled milk to blame for these thoughts.

Standing, she lowered her head and then, vertebra by vertebra, rolled down until she touched her toes. She let her arms go limp. Actors, the rejection experts, did this to warm up. She rolled up and felt her head swim. Courage could not be stretched or rolled into. She would just have to make the call.

"Fuckers. Scoundrels. Philistines. Assholes." Heart fluttering, she rang Marika.

"John Brady's office. Hi, this is Marika."

"Hello, Marika, it's Suzanne Foley returning your call."

"Yes, Suzanne. Been busy, have you?"

"Yes, I have." *You impertinent shite.*

"I have some news for you."

"Oh?" *Stay calm.*

"Remember Open House?"

"Yeah." *Christ, just say it.*

"Are you always that . . . boisterous?"

"I wasn't feeling well." *You haughty upstart. You dick-sucking girl Friday.*

"Mr. Brady remembers it."

"Mr. Brady, eh. Was he there? I didn't see him." *Why am I not talking to Frank?* "Why am I not talking to Frank?"

"Frank? This has nothing to do with Frank. Open House was not the success we had hoped it would be."

"Oh. That's too bad." *Here it comes.*

"But Mr. Brady will honour his promise."

"Promise?"

"Even though we only managed to sign up nine new ABS members at the Open House, you brought in the most."

"I *did?*"

"Yup. You signed up five."

"I *did?*"

"Yes. And because you signed up the most new members, you win the prize. You're going with Jason MacLeod on a business trip to Los Angeles . . . Suzanne? Did you get that?"

"Yes. I did," said Suzanne. "Thank you. When will this happen?"

"Next week. We've arranged your schedule with Frank, so it won't interfere with your membership writing."

"I'll think about it. No. Yes. No. Yes. No. Okay, I'll go."

"I'll email your itinerary. Congratulations."

"Yes. Thanks. Goodbye."

Suzanne hung up and looked into the tea mug, searching for leaves to read.

CHAPTER 19—WELLINGTON

The Foster Plan for Kids office in Edmonton was on Whyte Avenue. Suzanne stayed away from Whyte Avenue mainly because of its artsy cafés, lively restaurants and creative boutiques. Once in a while a show of sorts drew her to the neighbourhood, but on the whole she avoided the area, feeling unworthy to socialize with functioning artists. The office, on the second floor of a renovated historic building, had polished hardwood floors, high ceilings, big windows and an explosion of plants. A pleasant place to make a difference in a child's life. A woman of about fifty, wearing a long skirt and a sweater, walked by and smiled. She had a kind, soft face.

"I'll be with you in two minutes," she said. "Help yourself to some coffee."

"Where?!" said Suzanne, a little too enthusiastically.

"By the water cooler. I appreciate your patience."

"That's okay. I get it. I shill too. For ABS."

The woman paused, but then continued on. Suzanne poured herself a coffee and lounged on the worn couch in the reception area.

News of the Los Angeles trip had taken a day to settle in.

Two days later she had called Gordon.

"Just thought I'd let you know I'm not fired," she said.

"That's great news, Suzanne."

"Yeah. Looks like I'm going to Los Angeles with that troglodyte Jason."

"What?"

"I signed up the most new members and won. A little better than a T-shirt, I'd say."

Stunned but exhilarated, dumbfounded but apprehensive, she submitted to the invitation. She had never been to Los

Angeles before, and a quick jaunt to a warmer climate in the throes of an Alberta winter came as a welcome break. They were flying Air Canada and staying at a hotel somewhere. On whose buck she dutifully ignored. Although she'd be travelling with the very man who epitomized everything she loathed, she would dump him the minute they touched down on U.S. soil.

She had borrowed a travel bag from Wilma, who found a spare rummaging through her bedroom closet. "I'd lend you my Coors bag, but I might need it in case they keep me in the hospital. I'm scheduled for a lumpectomy on the twenty-seventh. Will you be around, in case I need you?"

"Sure. You're not lending me that bag you're holding up, are you?"

Wilma waved an Edmonton Eskimos gym bag. "That's all I got," she snapped. "Take it or leave it. Buy yourself one, you cheapskate. Where the hell have you been, anyway? If I didn't feel sorry for you I'd have told you to fuck off a long time ago."

"Stop feeling sorry for me."

Wilma shook her head. "I can't help it. You're pathetic. I'm the one with cancer and you're pathetic. You think you're smart. 'Educated.' But what do you *know*? Ah, forget it. Why am I saying all this?"

Head lowered, Suzanne chewed the inside of her cheek and picked at the crust on her hands.

"The Lord works in mysterious ways," said Wilma. She dropped the bag at Suzanne's feet. "So, are you doin' this guy or what? Why do you get to go to Los Angeles?"

"No, and I don't know."

"Are you still seeing that young boy? He's cute, but have some sense."

"No, and I know."

"You're weird, Suzanne. Just plain weird. Look, will you be going to Hollywood Boulevard? Can you pick me up a souvenir on the Walk of Fame?"

"I'll try to remember."

Suzanne watched Wilma kick a pile of clothes into the closet. Off guard and from nowhere, Suzanne felt strong affection for her.

Now, feeling unusually steady, Suzanne flipped through a catalogue of children from developing countries, mostly medium shots or long shots, one photo after another of an impoverished child, some smiling, most neutral. The catalogue reminded her of the talent catalogues producers used to cast for the occasional show at ABS. The headshots and credentials of hopeful actors, each vying for attention. *Pick me!* She wondered about the purpose of seeing the faces of dozens of poor children. How would she choose? By height, by weight, by nationality? By looks? Better they just assign her a kid. She couldn't imagine the kid would care where the money came from. *Just feed me and leave me alone.*

One picture caught her eye. A boy. He squinted at the camera and his arms were akimbo. Impressive pose. Commanding. She looked at the name and blurb beside the photo. Wellington Trumbo, age seven. Zambia. Parents dead. One sister. She looked over the picture again and the pose that said, *I'll get an education, go to the London School of Economics and return to Africa to implement business infrastructures*, or *I'll grow up, defy my teachers, join a mercenary firm and kill anyone for a price.* Or both. The kid had potential.

The kind woman with the long skirt and sweater returned to the reception area. "Sorry I took so long. Are you here to sponsor a child?"

Suzanne stood. She held the catalogue to her bosom and felt a surge of pride. Wellington would banish the past.

"Yes. Yes I am."

Chapter 20—Hotel Macdonald

John Brady ordered the medallions of beef in a jus reduction with baby vegetables, while Jason went with the sole vegetarian entrée, a risotto with grilled vegetables in a lemon sauce. Suzanne fretted over her decision, unused to fine creative cuisine. She abdicated responsibility to the server, asking him to "surprise her." She white-knuckled a glass of water and listened to the conversation between Jason and Brady. She vowed not to have a drop of alcohol. Amazed to have been invited for a meal with an executive, she sat back and kept quiet, figuring this tactic prudent.

"I feel lighter when I eat vegetarian food," said Jason.

"Do you find you get enough protein? You work out a lot," said Brady.

"I make protein shakes for myself. Whey powder. I mean, I feel sorry for animals. We boss them around."

"Are you a vegetarian?"

"No. Is that okay?"

The Harvest Room at the Hotel Macdonald hummed with subdued diners. Servers moved proficiently. The warm lighting and rich decor negated the wintry night outside.

Brady sipped his wine. "Yes, it's okay."

Suzanne had been to a few elegant old Canadian Pacific Hotel dining rooms with her spinster aunt. The aunt had taken it upon herself to be an etiquette coach for her brother's guttersnipes, but the task had proved futile, the children were too neurotic to tame. Suzanne sipped her water and surveyed the surroundings. The Harvest Room seemed the perfect space to contemplate the approach of middle age and a time of reaping what one has sown. She smiled to herself. Life past forty seemed unrealistic.

Jason bit into a roll and chewed. "I'm getting to like Edmonton. It's a nice town."

Brady locked eyes with Jason. After a few seconds, Jason averted his gaze to a businesswoman sitting at a nearby table.

"This is where you'll flourish," said Brady. "This is where your career will be made."

"I *did* win a Gemini Award once," Jason softly asserted.

Suzanne choked back water. "For what?"

"Hottest Newcomer: Voice/Commercial/Short/Long/Documentary/Children's Magazine Program or Series."

"What is that?"

"It's a category. I guess you wouldn't know."

Suzanne felt slighted by Jason's remark. She didn't know whether to retaliate with something snide or let the comment hang. A growing unease with the dinner knotted her stomach. It was one thing to agree to go to Los Angeles for some kind of business; fraternizing with the enemy was another thing entirely. She would strike no alliance. She wiggled her left foot under the table.

"Ms. Foley," said Brady. "I hear you made quite an impression on our guests at the Open House."

Her faced turned a mottled crimson. She wouldn't even try to excuse her actions. "All I can say is I'm sorry."

Jason folded his arms. Brady gestured for Suzanne to lean in. She tilted her head toward him.

"If you ever get that sloppy in public again, I'll personally kick your ass out the door."

"Understood," said Suzanne.

Jason tore another roll in half and slathered it with butter. Brady sat rail-straight in his chair. He placed his hands on the table, palms upward, ready to intone.

"This will be the last campaign for the current membership team. I can't believe they were allowed to sponge off the public purse for so long. Jason, you'll be ad libbing the next membership drive. We'll give you bullet points as reference. I mean, the inefficiency boggles the mind. Boggles. You. You have the look. The youth. They don't understand the business of television."

The server discreetly placed their entrees in front of them. Brady sliced into a beef medallion. He chewed his meat carefully. Jason fluffed the risotto with his fork. The server presented Suzanne with a fish fillet on a bed of lentils. He gave her a sympathetic nod and left them to their business. Suzanne's head whirled from Brady's words. She was part of "they," didn't he know that? Brady wielded his knife and plunged it into his meat. She guessed he was used to twelve-ounce porterhouse.

"John. I'm wondering," said Jason, smacking his lips and wiping his mouth with a linen napkin. "You were a documentary filmmaker for a long time. Do you miss it at all?"

"No."

"Is that so? Why is that?"

Brady chewed his beef and let out a moan of pleasure. He took a sip of wine. "I didn't want to tell stories any more."

Suzanne pursed her lips and sucked through her teeth, the way some Caribbean women did on the subway in Toronto. The sucking noise suggested many things—engagement, wisdom, disapproval.

"I lost interest in people a while ago," added Brady. "Systems, organizations, structures—they make sense." He smiled, eyes crinkling at the corners.

Jason grinned back. "Well. That's true."

"You know, Jason, I hand-picked you."

"Yes, you've mentioned that. Thank you, John. I appreciate that."

"And my wife. And selected others," he said. He turned to Suzanne. "Yes, Ms. Foley. I have plans for you, too. I have always been a shrewd investor."

She offered a tight smile and gave him a thumbs-up. The only way to wipe this meeting from her consciousness would be through alcohol poisoning.

"I have to turn this around," Brady said, determined. "ABS is a train wreck waiting to happen. No, it has happened, but no one seemed to care. Let the machinery rust. Let the body decay. Is that *decent*?"

"It doesn't sound like it is," offered Jason.

Brady shook his head. "I hate this country. Do you know what our national character is? Reticence. We should have joined the Thirteen Colonies while we had the chance. Never hesitate, even if it means you lose."

Jason nodded. "I agree with you. But by the Thirteen Colonies, do you mean, like, Rhodesia? Or Australia?"

Suzanne shot a glance at Brady. Their eyes met for a second. Brady dabbed his mouth with a napkin and kept going.

"I look forward to the day when Canadian identity as a policy is obsolete. And that's all I'll say tonight."

Flustered, Jason grabbed his water glass and raised it. "To the end of Canadian identity."

Brady chuckled. He raised his wine glass. "To the end of Canadian identity."

Suzanne could stand it no longer. She waved the server over.

"A beer, please."

CHAPTER 21—DOING THE HONOURABLE THING

With the business trip two days away and affairs with Colin still needing attention, Suzanne sought tranquility at a sacred place.

"You don't need shots to go to Los Angeles." Manny rested his head in his hands on the prescriptions counter and looked at her blankly.

"But I'd like to get shots," said Suzanne, "some kind of inoculation. The place devours more Canadians than Florida. I want to come back."

"Why do you come here begging for drugs?" He sighed.

"I am not begging for drugs, Manny. I'm just wondering what I can do to protect myself down there."

"Carry a gun."

"Now let's not stoop to stereotypes. I'm anxious, I suppose. You're a good friend—"

"Really?"

"Okay, maybe more like a fond acquaintance, and I'm looking for some advice. Encouragement, maybe."

Colin lingered in the background by the rack of condoms. From the corner of her eye she could see he was comparing different packages, reading the merits of each brand.

Manny rubbed his face and shifted his weight. It was 10:00 P.M. and the prescriptions counter was dead, except for Suzanne, who wrung her hands.

"You want to know what I think?" he said. "I think. Go. Just go. Enjoy. I've never been to California. Hawaii, yes. Warm weather is good for the bones. Go relax. The store closes soon."

"Okay, buddy. I'll go. And enjoy. If that's what you're prescribing. I'll do as you say. Because you know more than me at this point. But. I'll enjoy with caution. It will be a yellow-light kind of enjoyment. Thanks for everything, Manny. I'll see you upon my return!"

Manny had turned his back to her and walked away after he had said "The store closes soon."

She joined Colin, who still hovered by the condoms. His emerald eyes had edge. He grinned.

"These are ribbed," he said. "Supposed to increase sensation in the vagina." He nodded at the package, beholding it like a talisman.

He had gone from innocent to seamy in a matter of a month. He had bought new clothes for himself, ditching the checkered, buttoned shirts and corduroy pants for brand-name snowboarding gear. Baggy pants hung low and long T-shirts under short T-shirts became his style. Maybe one night she'd asked him to look like a snowboarding slacker, she didn't remember. Or maybe he'd initiated the change on his own, feeling a surge of youthful masculine prowess. No question he was beautiful, but she thrilled at the sight of him in his Home Depot apron, shirt buttoned to his neck, oozing self-consciousness.

"Do you need condoms?" she asked.

"Do *we* need condoms?" he said. "We're going to be out of them soon."

He slid his arm around her waist and kissed her. She tensed. So adolescent, kissing in front of the condom rack. So terribly and stupidly exciting. And why did they need condoms, when she was on the pill and he was a virgin? *Safety First* was his mantra. He'd learned that at Home Depot.

"No. Not here. Stop."

"What's the matter? Did you talk to your pharmacist?"

"Yeah."

She had it in her mind that she would break it off with Colin this night. But where? She couldn't decide on a locale. The pharmacy seemed as good a place as any. Over the phone was a particular favourite of hers. So was moving and not leaving a forwarding address. Because of the exceptional circumstances surrounding their affair, she felt she owed him a tête-à-tête. She might have to keep him from hitting his head or swallowing his tongue. A field seemed in order.

"Feel like going to the driving range in the River Valley?"

"The driving range. Why?"

Ten minutes later Colin leaned against the car with his arms folded while Suzanne paced the icy parking lot. He had been borrowing the family car lately, driving on his own for the first time. The thought of being behind the wheel of a car filled Suzanne with acute foreboding. She couldn't trust herself not to careen into other vehicles or floor it over a bridge. Not that she had that specific suicide wish. Burbling in some cranial recess was the idea that she'd walk away from a violent impact torn, bloodied and reconciled with the past.

"Feel like, I don't know, driving the car?" asked Colin, shuffling from side to side to stay warm.

"Uh, maybe not tonight, eh?"

They stood in the moonlight, two solitudes in parkas, the air a block between them. Snow, dry moisture, blanketed the field, its pure beauty parching. She looked at Colin, no longer as a plaything but as a young human being. He had *special needs,* whatever they were. All that was left was snow.

"What are we doing here?" he said. He went over to the driving range's gate and shook it. The clang ricocheted in the night.

She removed her hood and scrunched her face. "Colin."

"Baby, are you okay? Let's just sit in the car and go for a drive. Let's go back to your place."

She raised her eyebrows to stretch the tension from her face. She clasped her mitts. "Okay. Here it is. The fact of the matter is . . ."

"Is this about Los Angeles? Is something going to happen in L.A.?"

"No, it's not about L.A. Honestly, I have no idea why I'm going to L.A. This has come completely out of nowhere. John Brady has his own reasons." She could see his lower lip close to trembling. She sighed. "Colin. You're a great guy."

His voice wavered. "Yeah?"

"I'm a seriously flawed woman with many difficulties. Technical difficulties. I'm like a television receiving scrambled signals. Static. Permanent snow."

She stopped on the metaphor, knowing the imagery sounded crazy. "It has been my honour to, uh, show you the ropes and all. I like you. A lot. Might even love you."

"But?"

"But. Yes, there is a but. I think it would be in your best interests if we stopped seeing each other for a while."

"How do you know what's in my best interests?" he shot back.

The cold air made talking difficult. Her mouth began to gum up. "Look. You're . . . special. You truly are. You said so yourself. If it were up to me I'd marry you and provide for you. But. You have your whole life ahead of you. You're twenty. I'm . . . older than that. I'm finished. It's over for me. You have a chance. You should be hanging around people your own, um . . . age. I only say this because I care. Tell you what. Let me go to L.A., for whatever reason, and when I come back we'll talk."

His eyes filled with tears. He clenched his jaw. He pulled off his hood and smoothed his blond hair with his mitts. He stared down at the ice. The cold night creaked around them.

"Hey, uh. Can I get a ride home?" she asked.

He nodded quickly. "Yeah."

—

They sat in the car outside her apartment. He stared straight ahead through the windshield.

"Are you mad at me because I told you I went to a special camp?"

His insight caught her off guard. "Mad at you? I'm not mad at you."

He turned to her with a pitiful, fearful expression. "Don't go. It's not what you think. I'm different, that's all. That's what my mom says. I'm smart in a different way. Simple."

She closed her eyes and fought back tears. She knew his need, to be assured he wasn't a freak. Mr. Audi had done that for her. She'd tagged along with Diana and visited Mr. Audi for months. He'd paid Diana and the boy well for playing with him in his bedroom, showering them with clothes and gadgets. Every few weeks Diana would show up to school wearing new boots and lipstick. Suzanne became an expert forger, writing Diana notes for tardiness, copying her mother's signature with a steady hand, good enough to fool Mrs. Kelly, who knew that Diana's mother never went to high school. One night Mr. Audi had told Suzanne he was in love with her, which he explained meant a special connection. He'd pulled her shirt up and kissed her little breasts. "That's how people express love," he had said. She'd pulled her shirt down, feeling light-headed and queasy, cared for and sick at the same time.

"Please, Suzanne?" Colin prayed.

What was one more time? Simple.

Chapter 22—Love from Canada

February 5, 2001
Wellington Trumbo, c/o Sr. Maria Chabala
St. Mary's Motherhouse, Zambia, Africa

Dear Wellington:
Hi! My name is Suzanne Foley and I'm your new foster parent. I live in Canada, a very big country in North America. North America is north of Mexico, Central America and South America. Canada is north of the United States of America. Maybe you've heard of Canada. I bet you've heard of the U.S.A. It's hard to avoid.

Please find enclosed a pack of hockey cards. I hope you like the Montreal Canadiens. So, you go to school at the Motherhouse. What's your favourite subject? Do they teach you about God? Which God? Are the British out of Zambia for good? I looked up Zambia in an atlas and your national capital is Lusaka. Have you ever been there? Any good restaurants? Scratch that—I'm not supposed to compare my life to yours, sorry.

The atlas also says that nearly half the population of Africa is under the age of fifteen years old. Wow! You must have a lot of kids to play with. Zambia also has a lot of forest. Well, that's what the atlas says. Has it been clear-cut yet?

Canada is a big country with four seasons—winter, spring, summer and autumn. Our winters are very cold and snowy and last a long time and most people don't like it. I do. The bleakness helps me focus. No birds chirping or flowers blooming to distract me. Do you have snow in Zambia?

I hope my twenty bucks a month helps you out. I know it's not much, but I might be losing my job soon, so it's the best I can do. Don't spend it all in one place! (Although where would you spend it? The GAP? A video arcade? Ha!)

So, you have a sister! That's nice. I have three sisters and four brothers. I never see them. We all live far apart from each other. That's okay, it doesn't make me sad. We used to go skating and tobogganing (winter sports) when we were little, sometimes all night because my parents didn't want us in the house. That's why I like the winter. I had to.

What else? I hope you do well in school. I hope you have enough to eat and clean water to drink. I thank God every day that I have a roof over my head and food to eat. Okay, maybe not every day, but when I think about it, or when I'm in trouble. I liked the picture of you I saw at the Foster Plan for Kids office. You look like you mean business! Do you know that? You have your whole life ahead of you, Wellington. You have people around you who love you very much and they will help you grow up to be a fine young man. Are you named after the 1ˢᵗ Duke of Wellington, hero of Europe who defeated Napoleon at the Battle of Waterloo? Or Wellington, New Zealand? Or the boot? Maybe you're named after your Dad. Or maybe you're named after just you! Although, I bet some Brit foisted your name on you. They just can't seem to let go, can they? Don't get me wrong, I admire them enormously, but really, must their Queen be our Queen, you know what I'm saying? IGNORE THIS LAST SENTENCE.

Well, I'd better go. I'm taking a trip to Los Angeles, California, in the United States of America. I don't know why, I guess I won a contest. I'll send you a postcard from down there. I have to start packing. I go tomorrow. I don't know what to take.

Be good, Wellington. Know that I love you.

Your Foster Parent, Suzanne

P.S. Call me your Foster Buddy instead. I have never been a parent.

CHAPTER 23—AIR JASON

Thirty-four thousand feet in the air over Idaho and she declined, once again, an alcoholic beverage. Fists clenched and stomach in knots, she tried to relax to the "Sounds of Manchester" set list on an in-flight audio entertainment channel. Mozart wouldn't soothe the savage breast this time. Jason reclined in the seat next to her reading *15 Steps to Mastering Your Life and the Lives Around You*, a best-selling self-help tome.

The business trip hadn't alarmed her. The planning and execution of the itinerary proceeded smoothly. But now she understood her calm as a protective sensation like shock. Switching the music to Henry Mancini and gazing out the window at the purple and golden dusk, she felt very adult and very helpless. She had no true business visiting this city on the Pacific. She studied the flight course on the screen in front of her. The plane was over Idaho. Idaho. Idaho potatoes. Farmland and honesty. Humus.

She handled a glossy folder and read the cover. *The PBS Development Conference: Los Angeles Courtyard LAX Imperial.* When John Brady had explained that she and Jason would be attending a public television conference, Suzanne hooted.

"PBS? *The* PBS, as in the Public Broadcasting System? The American PBS? The PBS I used to watch from Vermont on UHS when I was a kid?"

"Yes."

"Wowee! But isn't PBS based in Washington?"

John peered over his glasses. "The conference isn't."

"Why us?" asked Suzanne, wide-eyed and grinning.

"Because I want you to learn from the pros. And I have to spend the money. Fiscal year end and all." She thanked him and was about to leave his office when he said, "Don't do anything untoward."

Now, beside Jason Macleod en route, Suzanne felt unaccustomed responsibility like a warm, nauseating flush. They were going to a PBS Conference. PBS—the *ne plus ultra* of publicly supported broadcasting, the big time. There was hope for her yet. She flipped through the folder and scanned the multitude of workshops and seminars offered: *"How Well Do You Know Your Viewers?"* *"Marketing Your Values."* *"What to Say and How to Say It: Pledge Messaging."* *"Major Giving Initiatives: Tools for Major Giving."* She gawked at the last workshop title. Major Giving. The only major giving that happened at ABS was when a nervous middle manager from Leduc Auto went on-air with Lawrence and presented him with a cheque for a thousand dollars. Not only did major giving happen in the United States, there were initiatives behind it. Were the Rockefellers still benefactors? Did they come on-air and present the membership host with a giant cardboard cheque too? She perused the workshops again. *"What to Say and How to Say It"* intrigued her. Did PBS use a more sophisticated language when it came to begging? Did they use adjectives she didn't? She removed her headset and smiled at a passing attendant.

"You know, I think I'll have a glass of white wine, if that's okay."

He poured some plonk in a plastic cup. "*Voilà, mademoiselle.*"

"*Comment ça va?*" she asked.

The steward launched into a barrage of French so rapid her eyes bugged. Twenty-three years of living in Quebec and the French language still eluded her. Fear of looking like an idiot kept her mute. Being an anglo didn't stop Jackie from functioning in Montreal, just kept her from any jobs over ten dollars an hour. Suzanne stared at the loquacious steward.

"*Alors,*" she said. "*Bien sûr.*"

Finally, he moved to the next row of passengers. She gulped the wine and fixed on the screen in the back of the chair facing her. Still over Idaho, over God-fearing folk and hardy crops.

She had gotten a lift to the airport from Colin. She'd let him stay overnight for convenience. In bed he had clutched her and twitched like a beaten pup. She allowed him to soothe himself by banging her savagely. Never having faked sexual pleasure before, she simultaneously moaned and winced. She stroked him mechanically, repulsed by her own cowardice. He climaxed twice and then immediately fell asleep, his breathing light and sweet. She spent most of the night watching his eyelids flutter in his sleep.

In the morning she had met Jason at the Air Canada ticket counter. He was looking polished in a light jacket, black trousers and grey sweater. He had checked one piece of luggage and carried a black leather tote bag. She had on a second-hand black cashmere overcoat, black pants, black sweater and a Montreal Canadiens toque. He acknowledged her and frowned at the toque. She hoped he wouldn't say anything about it.

"Hey, Suzanne. You gonna wear that?"

"Look. I know this sounds ridiculous, but this toque once saved me from certain death on a flight to Newfoundland. Just believe me."

"Whatever."

She felt she had to convince Jason that she wasn't being precious.

"No, no, I'm telling you. The captain got on the PA system and casually mentions to expect turbulence coming into Newfoundland. Something about shifting wind currents and crossing into different fronts causing little dips in altitude. No big deal, eh? Then right after his announcement, the plane drops like a baby from a bridge! Grown men and women start shrieking. The woman sitting beside me buried her face in a pillow. The only calm passenger I could see was a Catholic priest reading an article in the St. John's *Telegram*. All I could think of doing was to rifle through my bag and put my Montreal Canadiens toque. Understand that I was a kid in the glory days—Ken Dryden, Henri Richard, Guy Lafleur, Larry Robinson, Yvan Cournoyer, Serge Savard—they were real-life saviours who healed! I prayed to them for safety. And you know what happened? The turbulence stopped! And that's when I knew—the toque saved me. Saved us all!" Suzanne stopped speaking and stared at Jason. She instantly regretted saying anything.

He shrugged his shoulders. "Whatever. You still look like a goof."

Suzanne scowled and pulled the toque off, having no choice but to trust in the structure and design of Air Canada's fleet. She didn't want to get off to a bad start with Jason by telling him to fuck himself. Besides, she knew that he was right.

Now she stared again at the flight path on the screen. Still Idaho.

She popped the earphones back on. Stan Getz. A xylophone, the timbre of pixies, coaxed lunatic cravings for intoxicants. One more cutesy ding and she'd be jonesing for smack at LAX. She removed the earphones. *Change and take a chance.*

"Hey, Jason?"

Jason kept reading his book. "Yeah."

"Whatcha readin'?"

He tilted the cover toward her so she could read the title. She nodded. "I see. Is it good?"

"Uh-huh," he said, eyes on the page.

She gazed out at the twilight firmament, the cloak of the gods. *The cloak of the gods? For Christ's sake, relax.* She turned to Jason.

"Why?"

He grunted. "Why what?"

"Why? Why is the book good?"

"Because it's helpful."

"How so?"

He glanced at her and closed the book. He shifted in his seat, recoiling when he accidentally touched her thigh with his.

"Do you really want to know?"

"Yes. We have time to kill, so, yes."

"Let's say we have to go to a function at this conference."

"Let's say."

"There are two hundred people or so in the room. What's the first thing you'd do?"

"Head to the bar and try to find a TV set with a hockey game on."

"No. If you had known what the seventh step to mastering your life and the lives of others was, you'd know you have to go around the room and introduce yourself to people. You shake hands, ask questions. Mingle. Step Seven: Be Present. It's simple, just focus on the now without fear."

Suzanne picked at her fingernails. Maybe she had underestimated Jason. If this watered-down Buddhism shored him up and gave him a philosophical basis for being stupid, he could prove dangerous.

"Interesting. What's Step Eight?"

"Eat Breakfast."

"Right."

"Look," he said, "I know you don't like me."

She swallowed and jiggled her foot. He stopped at those words. He cracked open the book again. At least a minute passed before she felt uncomfortable enough to say something.

"What do you mean I don't like you?"

He looked at her accusingly. "I'm the new guard. You don't like it."

"Oh, that."

"You know who gets left behind? The people who can't change. Think about it. We're going to Los Angeles. Everything happens in Los Angeles. Movies, TV, everything. The possibilities are limitless."

"I hear you. But don't you find limitless possibility . . . un-Canadian?"

"Un-Canadian? Who cares? Why would you even think that?"

Suzanne tapped the PBS Conference folder. "Do you like public television?"

"I like *television*. Public, private—it makes no difference to me. When you're sick, what do you do?"

"What do I do when I'm sick?" Suzanne shrugged. "I don't know. Lie down."

"Exactly," said Jason. "People lie down. Then what do they do?"

"Just tell me."

"They turn on the TV. They don't go online or read a book. It's too much work."

"I read a book."

"That's you. The majority of people don't. They lie in front of the TV and watch whatever's on. Do you think they care whether it's public or private TV? They're too sick to care. Their bones and joints ache, their backs hurt, they have swollen feet, or gout or they're old or whatever. My job as a broadcast personality and actor is to keep people company. And more often than not, people are sick when they tune in. Sick one way or another. I know it and you know it. So why pretend we're anything more than that?"

Suzanne's nostrils flared. She stuffed the PBS folder in the storage pouch in front of her. Jason's attitude riled her. She wanted to shut him down, knock him out with a definitive observation. Instead, she reached down and pulled the Canadiens toque out of her carry-on bag. She slipped it on her head and hated that she understood him.

Chapter 24—PBS Conference: Courtyard LAX Imperial

She smoothed her only skirt, a dark-green plaid below-the-knee number, on the bed, hoping to have an opportunity to wear it and show off her newfound maturity. This clean and comfortable room delighted her. She had only stayed at a hotel on a handful of occasions. One time she'd had to console a distraught boyfriend who had spent two hundred dollars on the room only to be unable to perform sexually. On another occasion, the death of an aunt, the room in Halifax she'd occupied was rumoured to be haunted. Suzanne had spent the night listening to a broken tap drip.

This room at the Courtyard LAX Imperial had thick towels and bedding that promised "eternal" sleep. Even the wrongheaded promotion couldn't dampen her enthusiasm. Or concern. Why had she agreed to participate in this charade? For the experience, she reminded herself, to prepare for all the other charades in life to come. She examined her lily-white arms. More than ten minutes in the California sun would be metastasizing. She would get her sunshine at the La Brea Tar Pits, which she hoped to visit somehow. Maybe the hotel had a shuttle that stopped there. Otherwise she would roam the corridors and meeting rooms of the Courtyard LAX Imperial.

She surveyed the queen-sized bed. She pictured a male in the bed, but not the usual male. Not Colin, but Gordon. She felt his arms holding her. She let herself be held. She looked up at him with dreamy eyes, music filling her mind, cascading piano notes. *Pound me, Glenn. Forte. Fortissimo.*

The lonely bed beckoned her to wallow. Instead, she gathered her money and room key. There probably wouldn't be a library in the hotel, but there would certainly be a bar.

"Altitudes" attempted chic and achieved comfort. The blond wood, burgundy-shaded lights and taupe walls created an unintentional utilitarian effect. A large modern art print, a graphic mishmash, loomed in the centre of the dining area. An assortment of hotel patrons sipped their beverages at the curved bar, either waiting for a table or on their way to getting pie-eyed. Suzanne had every intention of not getting pie-eyed, but now, on her second glass of wine, she relaxed.

A woman sat next to Suzanne. She sipped a cranberry martini. She had dyed red hair and wore a blue scarf, a pale-blue knit sweater and a grey wool skirt. Suzanne guessed the woman to be in her late sixties. Her clear blue eyes were lined grey. Her face looked a little chalky from powder and her lips were coated a reddish-brown. Attractive now, this woman must have been a knockout in her youth. Suzanne felt magnanimous.

"Excuse me. Are you here for the conference?"

The woman smiled at Suzanne. "In a manner, yes. I am a friend of the hotel."

Suzanne nodded and took a sip of wine. This woman was a hanger-on. An elderly groupie. Her sweater set did look a little pilled. Still, the old girl carried herself with a sure sense of belonging. A horrid thought crossed Suzanne's mind. Was the old girl a prostitute? This was L.A., after all.

"I am also a friend of PBS," said the old girl. "Where are you from, dear?"

"I'm from Canada."

"Canada. You know Al Capone hid out in Moose Jaw for a while."

Suzanne didn't know that. "Is that so?"

"Yes. I had an uncle who worked with him."

Suzanne nodded to the bartender and he refreshed their drinks. This conversation showed promise, a pleasant change from arguing the fate of public broadcasting and whispering romantic doggerel to Colin.

"My name is Suzanne, by the way."

"Irene. Pleased to meet you."

They shook each other's small, delicate hands.

"Are you from Los Angeles?"

"Yes. I grew up in West Hollywood."

Suzanne couldn't help herself. "Wow."

"The city's changed quite a bit over the years," said Irene.

"Did you ever work in show business?"

"Sure. I was a script girl at Warner Brothers. I worked with Ronald Reagan once."

Suzanne sipped the fresh wine in front of her. This could have been Irene's only job ever in the entertainment industry and it evoked irrepressible awe. Her mind percolated with questions. If Irene had to drop a name, Reagan's was as good as any.

"I can't help but be impressed, Irene, even though I'm Canadian. American history is a lot of our history, whether we like it or not."

"Canada is a fine country."

Suzanne ruminated. The best name-dropping she could do in Edmonton was mention Cal Nagy at the local sandwich shop and hope the staff wouldn't spit in her turkey on whole wheat. But how often had Irene dredged up Reagan's name to try to impress a stranger in a bar or a surly store clerk, to try to gain some leverage? Suzanne felt obliged to take the onus off Irene.

"Carl Nagy likes to eat at the Brothers' Sandwich Shop on 116th Street."

Irene kept smiling. "Who?"

"Carl Nagy, one of the hosts of *This Day in Alberta*."

"Brothers' Sandwich Shop? In New York?"

"No, Edmonton."

"Oh, Edmonton. Who are your stars in Canada?"

"Well, our stars aren't so much stars as they are public servants. Anyone not comfortable with that usually comes down here and passes themselves off as American."

"Always have," said Irene. "Starting with Mary Pickford."

"That's right. And we celebrate them in Canada because they've left. But we don't celebrate too much. We celebrate in a sober, state-controlled manner. What we need now is a Ministry of Fame."

"I guess we can choose where we live, but we can't choose where we're born," she said.

Suzanne nodded and glimpsed at a chortling man behind them. With any luck we can choose where we die, she hoped. She felt programmed like a salmon to struggle upstream, go back, go back to the place of conception, of original sin, and die. For no other reason than to blot where it began.

"What's it like growing up where the weather is like a narcotic?"

"I've never thought about it that way. Lovely, I suppose."

Suzanne drained her wine and asked the bartender for a glass of beer. Time to switch up the beverage.

"Anything is possible down here, isn't it?"

"Anything is possible anywhere, my dear."

Irene smiled. She glowed with an august feminine charm. Suzanne wished Irene were her mother. Someone to listen to. And love.

"Did Reagan have political ambitions when you knew him?"

She laughed, sipped the crantini and winked. "He had ambitions, but I don't think we ever discussed politics."

Suzanne chuckled. Then, from the corner of her eye, she sensed a squat, blond-streaked presence. She glanced over at the entrance. Jason was sizing up the room. He looked over at the bar and met Suzanne's eyes.

"Damn!" she cried.

"Damn? Damn what?" asked Irene.

"Don't come over, don't come over, don't come over— DAMN, he's coming over!"

"Who's coming over? Red Rover?"

Suzanne sighed. "Just someone I work with, Irene. I'll only be a minute."

"That's okay. I have to be going—"

"No! Please stay. Don't leave me alone with—"

"Don't leave me alone with who?" said Jason, smiling. "Hello, ladies."

"Hello yourself," said Irene as she steadied herself on the back of Suzanne's bar stool. "I really must be going. There's a hospitality suite on the ninth floor I want to visit. KWPZ in New Hampshire. They make the best butter tarts. Goodbye to you both. I enjoyed chatting with you, Suzanne."

Jason gently guided Irene past him. He slid on the now-vacant bar stool. "Pretty hot babes at this conference," he said, and snorted.

Suzanne grumbled. She hoped he would be on his way soon, prayed he would make an ass of himself at a hospitality suite. The good citizens that ran PBS would detect an impostor, a slick charlatan among them, a flim-flam man. Hopefully they would ostracize him for the rest of the conference.

He ordered a beer and made a hissing sound. "I gotta get out of here."

"Yes, you do," she said.

Jason smiled tightly. "I'll be the one to decide." He sipped his beer and eyed one of the female bartenders.

"You think you're better than me, don't you?"

Suzanne looked at her wrist to check the time. She didn't have a watch on. "Do you have the time?"

"It's a quarter to eight. You really think you're better than me."

She sighed. "Why do you say that?"

"Because it's obvious. Because every time I'm near you, you tighten up. You're not better than me."

"I never said I was better than you."

"I climbed my way up, Ms. Foley. Came from nothing. Lived above a laundromat with my mother. I became an actor. Once in a while I got a break. And now here's another break. A potentially good break. I don't need you looking down your nose at me."

Suzanne shot him a look. "Yeah, well, don't fuck it up for the rest of us who came from nothing."

Jason pulled a bill out of his wallet and left it on the bar. "Same for me, babe. You know, I had you figured out. You're just like me."

Her nostrils flared. "I'm nothing like you."

"Step Ten: No One is Unique. Similarities bind us. Let's be civil to each other." He climbed off the bar stool. "Maybe I'll see you at a hospitality suite."

He moved in closer and whispered. "Let's make the best of it."

Chest puffed, he left the bar. She watched him enter the lobby and weave his way through packs of registering conventioneers. He paused to read the agenda for the conference on an announcement board. Two laughing women walked by.

"Room 1227! WKLT New Mexico. Come on up, sugar!" The women leaned into each other and whooped.

Jason smiled and spread his arms. "Well, after an invitation like that . . ." and followed them.

Now drunk instead of relaxed, Suzanne knew she had to leave the bar before she got to the point of no return. Jason had disarmed her with that last repulsive gesture. Any ill will on her part now would look petty. Why did he bother her so much? Her ideology had hardened her. Suzanne wished Irene would come back and tell her more stories about Hollywood. Maybe she could find Irene at one of the hospitality suites. Sliding off the bar stool, Suzanne went in search of Irene, friend of PBS and the hotel. She needed Irene in her life.

Chapter 25—Coming from Nothing

Thirty-two thousand feet in the air, returning to Edmonton with her brain and body dehydrated, she rehearsed in her mind what she would say to Jason.

I drink because it's the only thing that makes sense at the moment. And what else do we truly have but the present? I imbibe like a priestess communicating with the spirit world. Alcohol is a medium, a channel to a reality seen only by a chosen few. Good, I like that, that's good. Okay, where do prescription drugs fit into this? They . . . facilitate the transition, the transfiguration. Makes sense. I like that. I am bathed in light. It is the Grace of God. Yes. That is a reasonable explanation.

Now she had to convince Jason of this. Why Marika thought they'd be comfortable sitting next to each other on the airplane she didn't know. But there they were, the silence between them intense. She couldn't ignore it. Physically weak and emotionally raw, she needed reassurance, even if it was from someone she despised. She knew she still smelled from drink and vomit. *Well, let's just get it all on the table.*

How to explain the black eye when even she was unsure how she got it? Maybe he didn't notice it. What did she remember? She never did see Irene again. She remembered some of the conference.

She had attended two afternoon workshops. The first was called "How Not to Do an On-Air Pledge Break." The workshop leader presented a video clip from a pledge break produced by a PBS affiliate in Oregon. In it, a petite blond host interviewed a local zookeeper who handled a very large snake. The zookeeper invited the host to hold the snake. The host offered lighthearted protest, but allowed the zookeeper to place the snake in her arms. After a brief chitchat about the slithering reptile, the host and the zookeeper buckled down to the serious matter of discussing viewer-supported public broadcasting. As the zookeeper droned on, the snake began to wind its way around the host's shoulders. The zookeeper turned and addressed the camera directly, delivering a lengthy appeal to the audience, not noticing that the snake had wrapped itself around the host's neck. The host tried to pull the snake from her throat while continuing to smile and nod at the camera. Then she shrieked. Horrified, the zookeeper pried the snake off and the pledge break abruptly ended. Suzanne laughed longer and harder than anyone in the room.

"Don't book zookeepers with powerful reptiles," advised the rotund workshop leader.

Suzanne burst into more sustained laughter. A few people turned to see who was guffawing.

The next day, the second workshop, a hip-hoppish sounding topic called "*Churn vs. Flow*," was a discussion on audience retention between programming. She couldn't get into the "*Lunch with Marvin Hamlisch: New Approaches to Major Giving*" seminar, so she had to settle for a less glamourous discussion.

About twenty people occupied the large conference room. A panel of four producers sat at a head table on a raised platform. Two microphones were set up in the back of the room for questions. A producer asked the far-flung participants to assemble closer to the stage.

"One of the big problems we encounter as pledge break producers," began a panellist, "is how to segue smoothly from one program to another. We'd like to keep our audiences watching, but when we're coming out of a hard-hitting documentary and going into, say, a light comedy, our pledge break content requires a certain finesse. For instance, at WPTX Des Moines, we had to go from a pretty heavy documentary on child abuse to a Britcom, *The Vicar of Worthington Manor*. A one-eighty like this is no easy feat. Ideally we'd like to keep our viewers watching, but one audience is not the same as the other. This is 'churn.'"

Suzanne's face flushed. She wiggled her foot.

"How to do this? How to go from a harrowing story of inner-city poverty and sexual exploitation to the comical situations a port-drinking, card-playing, gluttonous vicar encounters is a delicate matter. You could even say a jarring matter."

Suzanne stared over the heads of the panel. Her hands clenched.

"Whereas 'flow' is when one program naturally gives way to the next. Two back-to-back comedies. A double-header of the same British drama, seamless. These breaks are easier to write and produce. The same audience. No heroic effort shifting gears."

That's all Suzanne remembered hearing. She suppressed paranoia. Why were these people talking about *her*? How did they know that that her life was constant churn, a difficult segue? She'd be the vicar of Worthington Manor instead of the subject of a documentary, a jolly sodden bounder instead of a victim. Suzanne glanced at the woman beside her. Did she feel the same mute panic?

Later that night, after doing the rounds at the hospitality suites and choking back dry hors d'oeuvres, an acute loneliness had overwhelmed her. She'd sat at the bar in Altitudes hoping to see Irene again. A bald man wearing a tan suit jacket sat next to her. She shifted away from him, inclining her head toward the door. She sensed his warmth and desire for a conversation. It made her sick. Loco-motion was taking over. Running out of cash, she lurched toward the elevator and the hospitality suites where free booze flowed. She hit the biggest hospitality suite of them all, WPTZ New York, and downed martini after martini with the hardcore sales reps. At that point in the evening the only people to witness mental and physical deterioration were the bartenders and catering staff, and they had seen it all.

She remembered the rough passage along the undulating corridor and dropping her room key. She'd woken up with her left eye throbbing. Maybe she owed Jason an explanation, maybe she didn't. She would give him one regardless.

"Hey, Jason." She tapped his arm.

He shifted his eyes from his book but didn't remove his earphones. "What?"

"I . . . About . . . Uh . . ."

Suzanne saw Jason's scowl. She would get no understanding from him. She pressed her right eyebrow with the palm of her hand. Did he see her that night? She squeezed her eyes shut to try to remember. Did he nudge her in the ribs with his foot? Did he dig his fingers into her shoulders and shake her? She looked over at him as he stared ahead. He hadn't shaved.

She decided she didn't want his understanding. She didn't need it. She was beyond his ability to comprehend. At ABS he was permanently out of his depths. She knew it and he knew it. She tapped his arm and he ripped his earphones off.

"What?!"

"I am a humble person."

"And?"

"That's all."

CHAPTER 26—SUNSHINE

A few days back from the trip to L.A., and she couldn't taste food. She had made herself a cheese and bacon sandwich for supper and decided to chew it slowly. She felt the runny smoothness of the cheese and the crunch of the bacon, but could not register anything salty or sweet or savoury. Her jaw moved, her teeth and saliva broke down the food, but there was nothing else. No lusciousness. No hit of pleasure.

To test her taste buds again, she dined at Teddy's the following night and ordered the curry of the day, a beef concoction with fresh coriander sprigs. Again, the usually fragrant thrill of turmeric, cumin and ginger was barely perceptible. She rolled the curry over her tongue and let it sit. All she could discern was pap. The next few days she hiked river valley paths, hoping the cold would invigorate her senses. Home in her studio apartment, brooding in front of the television, not having the energy to turn it on, she could only guess what little sensation she had in her mouth was a taste like machine water.

Suzanne took the bus over to the Home Depot to surprise Colin. She couldn't sever ties now. In the days leading up to the on-air membership campaign she needed to rely on this special boy for comfort and strength.

Cutting through the massive windswept parking lot, she gazed up at the starry night. There was so much mystery between heaven and earth, so much yearning, and the Home Depot sign, an answer to a riddle, lit the cold nothingness.

She headed to the Paint department and searched the aisles for him. She moved on to Hardware and Kitchen Appliances, ran a maze of microwaves, toasters, coffee makers, doorknobs, nails, screws. She doubled back to Paint. His sunny smile and hypnotic green eyes were nowhere to be seen. Puzzled, she busied herself with a colour wheel until she spotted one of his co-workers replenishing a row of tape.

"Excuse me, miss. Do you know if a fellow named Colin is working tonight?"

"Colin doesn't work here any more."

"What. Really? Since when."

"I think he quit last week."

Suzanne thanked the woman. She frowned and shoved her hands in her pockets. Shuffling toward the exit, she noticed a pay phone. She had to talk to him, to find out why he quit. Sorting through the surname Smith in the phone directory, she remembered that he lived on a street called Marlborough. She found an R. Smith on Marlborough. Suzanne dialled the number and held her breath, having never phoned him at his home before.

A woman, mostly likely his mother, answered the phone.

"Hello?"

"Oh, hello. May I please speak with Colin?"

"Who's speaking?"

She thought about giving a fake name. "It's Suzanne."

The voice on the other end turned sharp. "Don't call here again."

"I'm sorry?"

"You heard me. Haven't you done enough? You selfish, selfish woman!"

Suzanne tensed. "Haven't I—is this Colin's Mom?"

"Stay away from my son. You should be ashamed of yourself. He's a seventeen-year-old boy. He said you were twenty-nine!"

Suzanne struggled to speak. Seventeen? *He* had lied.

"Mrs. Smith, look, I had no idea—"

"Just leave him alone!"

"Is he okay? I mean, I—"

"How could you take advantage of him this way? I'll call the police if you ever see him again! He has amblyopia. Have you no shame."

"Amblyopia?"

"Yes, amblyopia!"

Suzanne stared at the sawdust on the floor.

"I'm sorry, Mrs. Smith, I really am. I had no idea. What—I don't know what that is—"

His mother hung up. Suzanne let the dial tone dissolve in her ear. Colin would be lost to her forever, cloistered in a suburban castle because he had amblyopia, whatever the hell that was.

She let the receiver sink back in its cradle. Who would be her sunshine now?

Wellington Trumbo, c/o Sr. Maria Chabala
St. Mary's Motherhouse PO Box 2202, Zambia, Africa

Hi Wellington!
Did you get my postcard from Los Angeles? What a place! I didn't see much of it at all. I was very busy working. But I can imagine its wealth and poverty. You see, Wellington, there's so much excess in North America. People live very, very well here, but they still complain. There are mortgages to pay, car payments to make, careers to advance, estates to plan, cottages to buy, kids to send to university, marriages to salvage, prolonged life expectancy. I don't have to worry about any of this personally, but I do. It's all around us, in our advertisements and reading material, constant reminders to need more, to expect more. I'm happy if I can wake up without a headache. That's a good day!

You know, Wellington—you're lucky. Lucky all you have to worry about is drinking clean water, having enough food to sustain you, and making sure you don't contract any infectious diseases. An education will fill your imagination and give you a love of knowledge. It will enrich your life and deepen it. But stay where you are. Be glad you live in a tiny village in Zambia. Stay there. Don't ever change.

One last thing, buddy. I'm up against an evil regime at my workplace. They want to privatize public television in Canada, kinda like private companies want to own all the water in the world. I can't let it happen. I can't let these crackpots take over. By the way, I can't taste food any more. No big loss, I'm a lousy cook.

Know that I love you. How's the twenty bucks a month working out? You're like a son to me, Wellington, the son I never had because I was too busy having fun and not thinking I'd live long. And to be honest, I just never thought it was in the realm of possibility for me. An asteroid hitting me has more of a possibility, and probability.

Love, Suzanne

P.S. Here's a picture of me with my best pal Jackie at beautiful Lake Louise in Banff, Alberta. I'm the one looking at my watch.

CHAPTER 27—WHAT'S PAST IS PRESENT

Slouched at a desk, Suzanne stared at a picture of Jason in the *Edmonton Journal*. Smiling, which made him appear more menacing than friendly, Jason had his arm around Rooey. Rooey's head dominated the picture, almost cutting Jason out of frame. The caption read "New Face of ABS Membership: Jason MacLeod." No clever puns or wordplay, just a bland identification lifted from an ABS press release. A couple of paragraphs described the February membership drive and the new vision for ABS. The reporter did a bit of editorializing, mentioning that the campaign target of one million dollars seemed "perhaps unrealistic." How a story about ABS membership got in the paper at all amazed Suzanne. Whatever PR machine John Brady had assembled seemed to break through systemic apathy. Still, the piece only consisted of two paragraphs, not the feature Brady probably anticipated. That made seeing Jason MacLeod's picture in the paper a little more bearable.

She gently touched her left eye. The swelling had gone down and the only evidence of foul play was a small yellowish tint above the eyelid.

This afternoon the library seemed particularly dull. Old European men studied foreign newspapers, some using them to jot down notes, their dialogue with the old country reduced to scribbling. The paper she had in her hands had a few illegible notes scrawled in the margins. She managed to decipher *facts are wrong* and *all are war pig*. A few old women with babushkas idled in chairs, bags by their swollen ankles. Suzanne squinted at the paper. The dim fluorescent lighting made reading painful. She went over to the newspaper stacks, and returned the *Journal*.

To the left of the *Edmonton Journal*, a few rows over and down, old copies of the *Montreal Gazette* collected dust. She paused and hovered over them. She rubbed her right eye. Sleep had escaped her for the last week. Every night the fall into unconsciousness terrified her. She avoided the Ativan, aware that she might get addicted. New and heavy nightmares along with the numb taste buds had begun shortly after she'd returned from Los Angeles. Black twisters loomed on bleached prairie horizons. Tornadoes transmuted into human arms and hands, whirling closer. The prairies curved and undulated, becoming flesh. A child's voice screamed "Let go!" and her eyes snapped open. Heart pounding, cold sweat soaking the sheets, she kept her eyes open, anything to avoid slipping back into the terror that lay beneath. She'd stuff it down. Will it down.

Hesitantly, carefully, she sifted through the *Gazette*. Not finding any copy from September, she asked the circulation desk. A desk attendant handed her a week's worth of old news from Montreal. Suzanne searched for a secluded chair and sorted through the days, scrutinizing the tragedies and the triumphs of the week. And then—Thursday, September 22, in section A, page 5—she saw the face of her molester, twenty-nine years later, Theodore Audi, arrested on charges of sexual assault, sexual interference, sexual exploitation and distribution of child pornography. If convicted, Audi would go to prison for a long time. She wondered who finally gave him up. Someone, now a courageous adult, had come forward. Could it have been Diana? The blond boy? Audi had made her a stranger to herself, a mute in relationships, and yet she'd chosen communications as a liveli-hood. Television: that reliable stream of images and sound, that comfortable reality. All her thoughts and hopes reduced to min-utes and seconds on a stopwatch.

Suzanne folded the paper, stacked it neatly with the others and left them with the circulation desk. She would have no con-frontation with him, would not come forward. Of all the adults she'd grown up with, he was the only one who'd had time for her. He had loved her, loved her sick.

She decided to phoned Frank. She had not spoken to him in an unnaturally long time. She dialled his number and looked out her apartment window to see a woman hurrying on the sidewalk wipe out on a patch of ice. She landed hard on her back. She did-n't move.

Frank answered the phone with a thin voice. "Hello."

Suzanne kept watching the prone woman, who remained still. "Frank? Is that you, Frank?"

"Yes. Hi, Suzanne."

A man in a puffy jacket came to the woman's aid. He knelt beside her. She wasn't moving.

"Thank God," said Suzanne.

"I aim to please," said Frank.

Suzanne cradled the receiver between her ear and shoulder as she opened the window. Cold air blew in. She saw the man outside talking on what appeared to be a mobile phone.

"Uh, Frank, there's something going on outside my window."

"It's called life, Suzanne."

"No. Never mind. Look, I've been emailing you scripts and you haven't replied."

"That's right."

The sound of sirens neared. The man crouched down again beside the woman and talked to her. She held out her arm.

"Have you *seen* the stuff I've written?"

"Yes."

"Are you going to let it go through?"

He paused. "Yes. All of it."

Suzanne white-knuckled the receiver. Frank was onside. Outside, an ambulance pulled up.

"That was fast. In Toronto you're lucky if you don't bleed out by the time they come."

"By the time who come?" asked Frank.

"Them. Sorry. Frank, are you okay?"

He cleared his throat and sighed. "I've been let go. This is the last campaign I work on. What else can I do? I devoted myself to ABS. I had beliefs. Where will I go? There's no place for me out there. What's going to happen to public television? To me?"

She held her breath and felt her beating heart turn brave. Outside, one paramedic attended to the woman while the other wheeled a stretcher to the curb.

"Frank, we'll rescue public television."

"Why bother? Nobody cares. Nobody cares about our jobs. Nobody believes in the public service, or even the public sphere any more. I'm tired, Suzanne. Really tired. I never told you this, but I enjoyed your scripts over the years. You have a way with threats and coercion."

A paramedic helped the woman sit up. The passerby remained at the scene.

"They took me to Los Angeles," she said. "Did you know that? I went with Jason MacLeod. I feel so cheap, so dirty. And why? Why did I go down?"

"I wondered that myself."

"The simple answer is, I don't know. They have plans for me. I'm hanging on like a rat."

"Like a rat? Better than glomming on like a zebra mussel, I suppose."

The paramedics lifted the woman and placed her on the stretcher. A few onlookers hovered. The man patted the woman's arm and the paramedics loaded her into the ambulance.

"Frank?"

The line was silent. He had hung up.

Suzanne put the receiver down. The paramedics slid into the cab of the ambulance. The onlookers and the man chatted with each other. He indicated the ice on the sidewalk.

She stood in front of the window, letting the cold air blow.

All of it, years of rationalization, of defence and flippancy and self-centred loathing, crystallized. No more wavering or seduction. She had given the interlopers a chance, but no more. John Brady and Jason MacLeod would go. She'd see to it. Jason MacLeod, the loathing she fought in herself, would go.

She vowed to be a rescuer instead of a victim.

Chapter 28—Natural Shocks

Pledge scripts somehow completed, rantings approved by Frank and inputted by the teleprompt technician, the only thing left to do was anticipate the disaster that would be night one of the on-air membership campaign. Dishevelled, dark circles under her eyes, Suzanne crossed Jasper Avenue and slipped into Teddy's to treat herself to a fortifying pre-show meal. She'd give it another go with her taste buds, maybe order chili and douse it in Tabasco sauce. She had considered phoning Gordon to join her, but felt shy. Did he know she found him attractive? Did she send out any signals? The only signals she knew involved aggressive proposition. Better to let him live in her imagination for now. Besides, the spectre of Mrs. Gordon loomed. Suzanne sat at the bar, ordered the chili and blew into her hands.

She glanced over at the booths on the upper level, up by the windows, the good seats, the romantic seats, and imagined herself there with Gordon. Then she spotted him. He had on a black T-shirt over a long-sleeved grey shirt and was smiling at a brown-haired girl sitting across the booth. She intertwined her fingers with his. He leaned in and brought her fingers to his mouth, kissing them lightly. He held her hand and took her in with smouldering eyes.

Colin.

"Fuck," she whispered.

She inched her way across the bar and scrounged for a newspaper, feeling the heat rise in her neck and ears. Her hands trembled as she sifted through papers. Tears in her eyes made it hard to see. She grabbed the Homes section and pretended to read about the latest in appliances.

She didn't know what to do. She dipped her fingers in a water jug behind the bar and ran them over her face to cool the redness. Colin's rendezvous with this young woman could be innocent, two friends just sharing a meal. The girl joined him on his side of the booth. He put his arm around her and said something in her ear that made her laugh. Suzanne sat straight on the bar stool, suddenly contemplating middle age. Wearing a tattered parka, second-hand boots, with greasy hair behind her ears, she watched Colin give the lovely girl a peck on the cheek.

Her cherished young man, the blond boy with the dreaded scourge of amblyopia, whatever the hell that was, now wore black and hung his arm around a female's neck like a gangster.

Colin took a sip of water and glanced toward the bar. He squinted. Suzanne let herself be seen. Their eyes met. She raised her hand in a feeble wave. He nodded and raised his hand quickly. His girlfriend looked around to see who Colin had acknowledged. Suzanne sat back down and returned to her chili and newspaper, stung, alone. She felt her abdomen bulge against her jeans, a roll of fat spilling over the waistline. She had never seen him wear black before. She sucked at some chili, fighting the urge to cry.

The honourable thing had finally been done. He had moved on.

Bloated from humiliation and lukewarm chili, she closed her apartment door. She slid off her coat and mitts, letting them fall in a dejected heap.

Where had Pauline been this whole time? What nonsense had she managed to write for the on-air campaign? She could use the reassurance of a female about now, a gentle voice and a kind spirit. Someone committed to doing the right thing and willing to make the sacrifice.

Suzanne rubbed her face and head and stood over the telephone. Sadness caught in her throat. The phone rang, starling her. She hoped it was Colin, ready to explain his infidelity.

"Hello?"

"Hey, freak. Where you been at?" asked Jackie.

Suzanne brightened a little at the sound of her pal's voice. "Heya."

"I tried calling yesterday. How was L.A.?"

"L.A.? Oh yeah, that. Sunny and depressing." Suzanne glanced at a picture of Wellington she had pinned on the wall by the window. "Guess what? I sponsored a foster child in Zambia, like you told me to do. Kid named Wellington. He's great."

"Good for you! Has he sent you a letter yet?"

"No. Maybe he's shy. He'll write when he writes." She decided not to tell Jackie about Colin. "What's going on?"

Jackie paused. "I have some news."

Suzanne grimaced at the picture of Wellington, proof of her attempt at normalcy. He squinted back. *I'm hanging on like a rat.*

"Remember Diana Perantozi? The kid who wore makeup in Grade Four? Your friend."

Jackie's words hit like a blow to the solar plexus. Suzanne's stomach clenched.

"Look, Jackie, I can't take it. I can't hear that name right now. Not that."

She squeezed back tears. Guilt and shame cut behind her eyes. She had failed Diana. She'd managed to talk herself out of Audi's picture catalogue, a bit shrewder than her less fortunate friend. When Diana cried and pounded on walls after a photo session at Audi's, Suzanne made jokes, mimicking the comedians she saw on television to make Diana laugh. Told her it was all in a day's work, a job. Diana had to help feed her brother and sister, after all.

She had failed Diana. Diana must have come forward, made a statement, and then taken a header off a building.

"No. It's good news. I saw her at the Cavendish Mall the other day. She recognized me first. I haven't seen her since grade school. She looked great."

"Yeah?"

"Yeah. She was shopping for shoes with her sixteen-year-old daughter. Mentioned that she talked to the police about Audi. She's been through the wringer in her life. She asked about you. She actually said 'God bless' to me as I said goodbye. God bless."

Suzanne glanced toward the kitchen, at a half-eaten sandwich on the counter. "Really? That's . . . amazing."

"Her daughter is gorgeous."

"Amazing."

"That's not all."

Suzanne sensed Jackie was smiling.

"Get ready for this," said Jackie. "You're going to be an aunt again."

"I already am an aunt, seven times."

"No, Suz, I'm pregnant."

Suzanne felt confused. "Pregnant? How? I haven't been to Montreal in over a year."

"You don't need to be here for me to get pregnant."

She stammered a reply to Jackie's revelation. "Pregnant? With a baby? What?"

"I had to wait to tell you. I can't believe it."

Suzanne forced a smile. She tried to disguise self-pity. "Great," she said, her voice high and wavering, "a baby. And you want it."

"Oh course I want it! What choice do I have?"

"There's always a choice," she muttered. "That's . . . good news, Jackie."

Jackie snapped. "Be happy for me, will ya? Just try."

Tears welled in Suzanne's eyes. She didn't want to alienate her best friend. *Pass the tartar sauce old chap!* "I am, Jackie. I am. It's just a little surprising, that's all. But it's wonderful news. News I am not accustomed to hearing."

Jackie sighed. "Okay. That's better. Thanks. Everything will be okay. Everything is okay. Let's talk later. I guess you need this to sink in."

Suzanne hung up the phone and leaned on her desk for balance. Jackie's good news felt like an assault. Suzanne reached for some Ativan. She shook a few into her palm and then a few more. She ran a tap in the kitchen and slurped them down. Instinctively, automatically, she scavenged for boots and coat. She had to go out, to move.

The Fellow was curled up in the vestibule, intent on hiding the bottle in his jacket. The vestibule offered him a haven from the deadly frozen night only a door away, only a complaint from a tenant away. She pulled the apartment building door open, teetered on the landing, and stared into the pressing darkness beyond the exit door. Suddenly a thought occurred, a duty. *Check the mail.* She groped for her keys and leaned into the mailboxes. There was a letter in her box. She ripped it open.

Missus Suzanne
Edmonton, Canada

Hello:
This is from Wellington in Zambia, Africa. Thank you for the honkey cards. They are nice. I have been in school and play. We thank God. Your letters make me sad. Be light! Do not be heavy in your heart. I hope God blesses you.

From Wellington

p.s. I have a shirt that has GAP on a tag.

Suzanne folded the letter and stuffed it in her pocket. She felt her knees buckle. She bumped against the radiator and fell to the floor. She sat and leaned against the wall, smiling at the Fellow.

"Hey. Mr. Fellow. Buddy. Guess what? I'm celebrating. I've had some good fucking news. Can I just sit with you? It's cold out. I'm getting tired. Can I have some of what you have? You and me, huh? Just a bit."

He grinned, revealing his rotten teeth, and mumbled. She reached over and snatched the bottle tucked in his jacket.

"Don't worry." Head swimming and eyes heavy, she scanned the bottle, its contents a clear liquid. "It's okay," she said to him. "You're okay. I know you are. Cheers! A toast! We're celebrating. Yes the fuck we are."

CHAPTER 29—CRUSADE

Her eyeballs darted. She tasted ore. An altar. She flailed under Jason. He rubbed her throat and wrapped his hands around her neck. He knelt on her chest, smiled and squeezed. His eyes rolled back, he screwed up his face and grunted.

She jolted awake. Blackness whirled. She rolled onto her back. Nauseating pain radiated through her body and head, terror clenched her heart. Objects began to come into focus. Chair. End table. Phone. Alarm clock. She looked at the time: 6:40. She squeezed her head. Throbbing pain pounded against her skull, a parched mouth and esophagus made her gag. She rolled off the bed and stood. Dizzy and weak, she flopped back down. She raised herself up on her elbows and stared into the darkness.

Swallowing back a rush of vomit, she reached over and switched on the bedside light. Her eyes felt swollen. Had someone beaten her up? She grabbed the phone, needing to talk to someone. Trembling, she pressed out Gordon's phone number. An answering machine invited her to leave a message after the beep.

Suzanne cried into the phone. "Gordon. Gordon. It's me. Suzanne. You work with me. I, uh, I need, uh. I don't know. Help me. God . . . is the campaign—"

A loud squealing sounded as Gordon picked up his phone. He shut off the machine. "Suzanne? Hi. What's going on?"

"Gord, is it morning or night?"

"Morning or night? It's Friday evening, around quarter to seven."

She guessed she had been unconscious over twenty-four hours. "Fuck. I'm in agony. I think I have brain damage."

"What's wrong? I'll come over right now if you want."

Her stomach pumped again. Hot vileness shot up. She swallowed it back. The instinct for survival, however feeble, overcame. He was her lifeline.

"Suzanne."

Her thoughts started to clear. "Friday. It's Friday? Tonight's the first night of the campaign! Shit! Fucking shit! Jason will be reading my script!"

"Yeah. It's finally happening. I'll come over, right now."

"Christ! I gotta get there! I wanna see him go down! I've been waiting for this, living for this!"

"We can watch it on television. Together. I'll come over."

"I gotta go! Meet me at ABS. It's time to move on!"

She hung up and sprang from the bed. Vomit gushed. She covered her mouth and staggered to the toilet, thin puke and blood leaking from her hand. She heaved her stomach contents, gut pumping violently. Quivering, she wiped her mouth and spun around to find some clothes. She pulled on something black and headed for the kitchen. She gulped water from the tap.

Frantic, barely able to see straight, she charged down the hall and pounded on Wilma's door. Suzanne could hear Wilma lower the volume on the television.

"Just a goddamn minute," Wilma barked. Lethargic steps neared and locks were unfastened. Wilma opened the door a crack.

"Oh. YOU." She opened the door wider and waved Suzanne in. "What the hell is the matter with you? Do you want to get yourself evicted or something?"

"No time for that. Get your coat on now!"

"Get my coat on? What the hell are you talking about? You need to sleep it off. What's the big idea passing out in the vestibule? Me and the super had to haul your sorry ass up the stairs and dump you on your bed. You want people to start talking? Keep it up."

"Yeah, yeah. Hurry, there's no time to lose." Suzanne handed Wilma her coat. "Can I borrow some toothpaste and some aspirin?" She headed for the bathroom.

"I guess so. Look, I feel pretty shitty tonight. The chemo is making me really tired. Although I look better than you right now. I don't want to go out."

Suzanne opened Wilma's fridge and grabbed some bottled water. "What are you doing with bottled water?"

Wilma folded her arms. "It's my new health regime. Try it sometime."

Suzanne guided Wilma toward the closet by the door. "You have to come out. You're going to be on television."

"I'm going to be on television?" said Wilma flatly. "Right. Me and the King of Kensington. You're nuts, you know that?"

Suzanne held Wilma's coat for her and slid her arms inside. "You're going to help save ABS."

Too stunned to resist, Wilma let Suzanne bundle her up. "ABS? The place you work?"

"Yes. I need you to answer phones. On TV." Suzanne unzipped Wilma's boots and slipped them on her puffy extremities. "Tonight, you will be seen by millions."

"Millions?"

"Okay, thousands. Maybe hundreds. You're going to be a part of history."

Wilma looked dazed. "I'm going to be on TV? I should phone someone." She clutched her chest, her breathing shallow. "I don't feel so hot."

"Don't worry. You'll be fine. You're doing a tremendous service for the people of Alberta."

Suzanne opened the door for Wilma, who shuffled into the hallway. "All right, I guess. Get my purse, will you?"

"Don't ask questions. Just do what I say and everything will be all right." Suzanne lost her balance and crashed into the wall.

Wilma shook her head and went to retrieve her purse. "You might need a shot to keep you steady, kid," she said, producing a mickey of rum. "I'll keep it, just in case. Have a snort."

Suzanne blinked at the bottle and felt the scorch of dry regret in her mouth. "No. Ugh. God, no. Let's go. Hurry."

In the vestibule, the Fellow leaned near the door, appearing alert and ready to flee at the first sign of trouble. He weaved in place and tried to be inconspicuous.

Suzanne nodded vigorously. "Yes. Yes. You too. Fellow." She stretched out her hand and placed it on his shoulder. He looked ahead, but tilted his head toward her.

"Mr. Fellow. I apologize for never learning your name, but how would you like to come with us and have something to eat? Get out of the cold for a while. I'm sorry if I imposed on you the other night when I passed out. That wasn't polite. You were very kind to share. I don't remember. I feel very sick."

"Are you crazy?" said Wilma. "Don't invite the Newfie!"

He shifted his weight and shyly glanced at Suzanne. She smiled at him. "Trust me. Have some food."

He nodded. "Okay." He snapped up his Eskimos jacket and followed Suzanne and Wilma out the door.

They stood on the corner of Jasper and 114 Street, the winter night deep and freezing and still. Across the street, Teddy's beckoned. The occasional car rumbled by.

Wilma began to cough and wheeze. She closed her eyes. "I don't feel so hot."

"Okay. Here's what we'll do." Suzanne gathered them in a huddle, addressing them like a coach. "No waiting for a bus tonight. Let's hail a cab."

"A cab?" said Wilma. "Nobody just 'hails' cabs. How long have you lived in Edmonton?"

Suzanne nodded. "Right. Okay. Wait here. I'll be right back."

She left her charges on the street corner and rushed into Pharmasave. She hurried toward the prescriptions counter, bellowing. "Manny. Manny, buddy! Could you please call for a taxi?"

Manny and Sabrina were quietly preparing orders. He raised his head from the pill bottles. Suzanne leaned over the prescriptions counter. Manny scowled. "What do you want?"

"I need a cab. Now. Please help."

Sabrina rolled her eyes. Manny stopped what he was doing. "Do I look like a . . . taxi guy whatchamacallit dispatcher? Use the pay phone!"

"Please. It's an emergency. I'll be outside."

He looked at the rash around her eyes and couldn't ignore her agitation. Her mouth hung open. He sighed and nodded at Sabrina. "Would you mind calling Miss Suzanne a cab?"

"Thanks, Manny. You're a lifesaver."

As Suzanne hurried away, he called after her. "Stop doing what you're doing to yourself. I'm tired of it. And you'll be dead."

Wilma and Mr. Fellow hadn't budged from the street corner. Under the street light they looked almost romantic together, their icy breath a conduit.

"Okay, I had the pharmacy call a cab for us," said Suzanne, "everything's under control."

"Why are we standing out here?" asked Wilma. "Let's go inside for Christ's sake and warm up."

"No time. No time."

The humane sight of a glowing taxi sign approached.

"That's us, gang." Suzanne walked into traffic and waved her arms. A car swerved to avoid her. The cab screeched and pulled over. Wilma and Mr. Fellow climbed in the back while Suzanne slid in beside the driver.

"That wasn't too smart," he said, "you coulda got killed."

"The Alberta Broadcasting System, please."

"Out on Stony Plain and nowhere?"

"That's the place." Suzanne pulled out a bottle of water, a toothbrush and toothpaste from her coat pocket. "Don't mind me, sir, I'll be careful." She quickly brushed her teeth.

The cab driver grimaced. "Hey! Don't gob on anything."

She scraped her tongue, rolled down the window, leaned out and spat. "Better."

"I can still smell the booze on you," he said.

She was about to retort but kept quiet. She knew the smell of her slow death hung in the air.

Chapter 30—Please Stand By

Bursts of ABS-branded balloons festooned the small lobby. Signs with arrows pointing down the stairs led ABS volunteers to a green room and the on-air membership campaign HQ. Two elderly greeters wearing name tags looked concerned as Suzanne, Wilma and the Fellow rushed past.

"Excuse me. Hello?" said a greeter.

Suzanne flashed her ABS ID at them and continued down the stairs. The ID was a new measure introduced by John Brady. Over her ID photo she had taped a picture of a computer.

"It's okay, ladies, I'm an ABS freelancer. Really. These people are phone volunteers. Call Frank in the studio if you need to." Her voice echoed down the stairs. "Thank you for your time and dedication to ABS. We couldn't continue without you."

The basement buzzed with the reedy excitement of an opening night. An assortment of volunteers, most of them regulars, shuffled and scurried down the corridor. These people had a fanatical devotion to ABS: elderly women, awkward and solitary middle-aged males, the mentally challenged, the physically challenged, the emotionally challenged and the challenged in general. Suzanne wheeled around a corner and into an excruciatingly fluorescent-lit lunchroom. A cluster of volunteers eating cookies and playing cards sat around a table. In a corner, ABS programming droned on a television monitor, a grainy, colour-faded documentary about marmots. She recognized several volunteers from campaigns gone by, when she'd drop in occasionally to gorge on the excellent craft services provided by one of Edmonton's top caterers.

"Hi there," she said. Looking around, she noticed there was no food, no spread. "Where's the food?"

Mildred, a large woman in her sixties who liked to complain about the arthritis in her hands, pointed to a couple of grease-stained fast food buckets on a counter.

"Fried chicken? That's it?" said Suzanne.

"And fries," Mildred drawled, shifting the cards in her hand.

Wilma and the Fellow had followed Suzanne into the lunch-room. A couple of the volunteers glanced at them haughtily. The Fellow leaned in the doorframe. Under the glare of the fluorescent lighting, his appearance was macabre. He smelled of urine and decay. Suzanne pulled up two chairs for the Fellow and Wilma to sit down.

"Say hello to our newest ABS volunteers, Wilma and . . . Fred. They'll be manning the phones at the eight o'clock break."

Among this collection of fringe players, there was still a pecking order. Mildred rolled her eyes and tossed down a card. Harriet, a well-groomed woman whose trademark was yellow shawls, folded her arms.

"*He's* not appearing on camera looking like *that*, is he?"

"Like what?" asked Suzanne. "A Newfie? An eastern bum and creep?"

Harriet took visible offence. "That's *not* what I mean."

"Fred here is a writer. He's been working very hard on a novel. I'm sure, as a woman who appreciates the artistic process, you understand how details like hygiene might escape his mind at times."

The Fellow drooped over the chair. He pulled a mickey from his jacket pocket and took a swig.

Wilma shrugged and looked around at the volunteers. "I don't know him," she said.

Suzanne reeled. Her brain and mouth burned. The only thing propelling her was mania. She opened the fridge and grabbed some juice. She guzzled a bottle of juice, then handed some to Wilma and the Fellow. "Help yourself to whatever's in those buckets. I have to go to the studio. How did the last break go, Dave?"

Dave, a man with cerebral palsy, confined to a wheelchair, showed a faithfulness to ABS that was truly touching. He had a mischievous sense of humour and could always be relied on to chitchat about the other volunteers. She knelt down beside him to hear his response.

"Nnnooottt ssssssooooo ggooooodddd," he said.

"Dave, can you keep an eye on my friends for me? Show them the ropes? They're newfies—I mean newbies. ABS keeners."

Wilma picked at the remainders in one bucket. The Fellow had the other bucket cradled in his arms. He tore into the chicken, skin and bones hanging from his open mouth. Harriet shuddered.

Suzanne whispered to Wilma. "I'll be back. Take care of Mr. Fellow."

"I'd better be on TV because this sucks. I don't feel too well. Do I get makeup?"

Suzanne hurried out of the lunchroom and into the studio. Two cameramen were off to the side reading the *Edmonton Sun*. The set—a podium and a riser where ten phone volunteers answered calls—blazed under the lighting grid. The next pledge break was ten minutes away but phone volunteers scrambled to keep up with ringing phones.

To the right of the set, Jason, wearing a boxy suit and shiny tie, gesticulated madly at Frank. Frank nodded and tapped the clipboard he held. Suzanne stood back in the dark for a moment and listened.

"You have to change this now, Frank! These people want my blood! I had no idea anyone even watched this station."

"They watch to complain."

"I'm trusting that what I say is correct!"

Pain shot through her head, from the back of her skull to the top of her scalp, and then stabbed behind her eyes. Her vision blurred. She scrunched her eyes and took deep breaths. She couldn't watch Jason harangue Frank any more. Her heart skipped and thumped. If there was any reason for her malignant self-affliction, her pathological drunkenness, it fumed and wrung its hands close by. That Neanderthal in the off-the-rack suit and Brady, his dark overlord of a boss, defiled the purity of the ABS *body*. Their stupid, nearsighted views, their grasping, greedy hands *molested* that body. She swallowed and ambled over to the men, stuffing her trembling hands in her pockets to hide them.

"Hello."

Jason gawked at her. "What are *you* doing here?"

"I wrote tonight's script. How's it going?"

Frank smiled at her, then frowned. He glanced at his watch and walked away. "Five minutes, guys."

"Yeah, tonight's script," said Jason curtly, "about the content. It's upsetting people. Why?"

"I don't know."

"What do you mean you don't know? You wrote this."

"In an effort to communicate. Ad lib, if that makes you more comfortable."

He waved a script at her. "This is tomorrow night's show. I'll just read this. There's no swear words in this one. Why would you write 'Eat the rich and fuck the poor' anyway?"

She glanced at the name on the script he waved. Pauline.

He bared his teeth. Sweat beaded through his makeup. "I won't read anything else that's offensive or false."

"Suit yourself. Can I take a look at the other script, please?"

Jason shoved the paper at her. Suzanne skimmed the first page. All reasoned, provincial government–approved argument straight from the ABS policy mandate, flat and courteous appeals for donations. Suzanne gaped. Pauline had double-crossed her. Pauline, the woman she'd had lunch with, the woman she'd looked to for reassurance, if not lesbian inklings, had lost her nerve. Unless Gordon had submitted careless, non-factual copy, she would be hung out to dry.

The cameramen put down their newspapers and waddled back to their machines.

"Two minutes!" shouted the floor manager.

Fresh phone volunteers began to file in to replace the ones that had handled the last flurry of calls. Suzanne crowed when she saw a confused Wilma and Mr. Fellow straggle in. Someone had plastered bright colours on Wilma's cheeks, eyes and lips. Mr.

Fellow had his hair combed back and his face was matte with powder. He stood at the side of the set looking frightened. Suzanne rushed over.

"Wilma. Why don't you sit next to Mildred. Fred, why don't you sit by the edge of the set, next to Dave."

Mr. Fellow shook his head. "Don't want to."

"Look, there's nothing to worry about. I'll buy you a 40-pounder right after this. I promise. Trust me. You're helping. You'll be okay. I know you're okay." She escorted him to a chair. "If the phone rings, pick it up. That's all you have to do."

Dave ran his motorized wheelchair up a small incline and settled in behind the table. "Dave, can you reassure Fred here that he'll be fine," she asked.

Dave gestured for Suzanne to move in close to him. "Ttthhhaattt ggggguy is ffuuuccckkked uupppp," he said.

"ONE MINUTE."

Wilma sat next to Mildred, who turned her back and chatted with Harriet. Wilma barked at Suzanne. "This is bullshit!"

Suzanne flinched and moved over to Wilma. She patted her hand. "Wilma, this is television. Of course it's bullshit. The bull-shit we love."

"No. These broads are bullshit. They're jealous I have ABS connections."

"Pay no attention to them. Now, when the phone rings, pick it up. That's all you have to do."

"What do I say?"

"Whatever you want."

"Your nose is bleeding."

Suzanne wiped her nose with her hand, blood streaking her wrist.

"THIRTY SECONDS!"

Suzanne squeezed the bridge of her nose and tilted her head back. A couple of the phone volunteers noticed and whispered. She moved out from under the stage lights and found a tissue box.

"Those tissues are mine," said Jason.

"TWENTY SECONDS!"

Blood leaked from her nostrils. Suzanne pressed some tissues to her nose. "Have a good one, Jason."

He saw the blood and stood back. "What the hell is wrong with you?"

"Remember, feel free to ad lib."

"TEN SECONDS. NINE . . ."

Jason took his position behind the podium. He animated his face to Camera 1. Suzanne left the studio, holding the tissues to her nose. She kept her head down to avoid alarming anyone. She ducked into Dressing Room 2 and closed the door.

On the counter by the makeup mirrors a monitor flashed the ABS titles. She tossed a pile of men's dress shirts off the couch and lay down, elevating her head on the armrest. Blood continued to flow from her nose, soaking the tissue into a soggy ball. She reached down, grabbed a dress shirt and pressed it to her nose.

Up came Jason and the studio on the monitor. The ABS public television membership campaign for February was on the air, live.

CAMERA 1: JASON:

I hope you enjoyed tonight's episode of Creatures Large and Little. *I didn't know the marmot was a squirrel, did you? Well, I'm from Toronto, I don't know much about anything north of the 401, west of Mississauga or east of Scarborough. I think there's a lake somewhere . . . Marmots apparently are gregarious rodents. Sort of like myself—*

Jason cut himself off and smiled uncomfortably. He forced a chuckle. Suzanne glanced at the clock on the wall in the dressing room. Another eight minutes to go. She squeezed the shirt to her nose, feeling light-headed. On TV, Jason glowed, as if from radioactivity.

Now, before we air Inspector Callaghan *I'd like you to pick up the phone, dial 1-800–555–1212 and give us your money.*

Give us your money. Your money. Your cheque, your money order, your pre-authorized credit card payment. Ignore the other charities: the sick kids, the emaciated adults, the shivering homeless, the abandoned animals, the depressed artists, the lost youths, the lonely immigrants, the bankrupt farmers. What do they do for you? Do they entertain you? Do they bring you hours of uninterrupted high-quality television programming?
Do they make your kids laugh?

One by one the phones started to ring. The image cut from Jason's puzzled expression to a pan of the phone volunteers. Wilma smiled and waved at the camera, while Mildred reached over and picked up Wilma's receiver, handing it to her. Mr. Fellow slouched in his chair and dragged from his bottle. Dave valiantly poked at Mr. Fellow's ringing phone, dislodging the receiver from the base. The image cut abruptly back to Jason. He reeled off his lines from the teleprompter:

Give us your money. Now! Don't ask where it goes. You don't want to know. We say programming, but how do you know for sure? Why am I saying this? There's new management at ABS. Did you know that? I'm the new face of ABS. This is it. Say goodbye to decency and polite discourse. To sincerity and purpose.

"That's it! I'm not reading off the prompter any more!" Jason waved his arms in protest.

The television image cut to a close-up of a grave-looking Mildred engrossed in conversation on the phone. She mouthed the words "I'm sorry" several times. The murmur of the phone volunteers grew louder and more staccato. The image cut to a wide shot of the set, Jason off to the side wringing his hands.

A cameraman shouted "AD LIB" and "ROOEY'S COMING." Jason plastered a smile on his face and continued:

So, keep those phones ringing, folks, we need to raise a million dollars . . . or else . . . I bet the programming on ABS keeps

you watching, uh . . . Inspector Callaghan *is on next. It's
one of our most highly rated shows. I'm not sure what the numbers are exactly.*

Suzanne gloated at the catastrophe. The image cut to Wilma
yelling into her receiver and slamming it down. Then a quick cut
to Dave's bent head and twisted mouth. Then a quick cut to a
pan of the volunteers frantically jotting down notes. Then a
quick cut back to a beleaguered Jason, gawking at the volunteers.
He pivoted and faced the camera:

*Look at these people who've volunteered their time to be here.
I mean . . . just look at them.*

Jason swept his arm to indicate the volunteers. Mr. Fellow
was face down on the table. Jason shot a glance at his watch:

*Only . . . four more minutes to go until we bring you the next
show. Yup, only four more minutes . . . okay, now it's about
three minutes forty seconds . . .*

Suzanne heard frantic shouts and rushing in the corridor. She
stopped applying pressure to her nose and looked at the balled,
bloodstained shirt. The nosebleed was not going away.
Back on the television, Jason smiled and shook his head:

*Folks, we are listening to you when you call in, believe me. But
please remember to pledge an amount of money when you do call
in. Let's just calm down and proceed with the fundraising . . .
Where's Rooey? I said, WHERE'S ROOEY?*

Jason swung around in search of someone to bail him out.
The camera panned over to reveal Leslie in the corner in full
Rooey costume, except for Rooey's head. When Leslie saw that
he had accidentally been caught, he stared into the camera. The
image cut back to a bemused Jason.

That, uh, that . . . wasn't Rooey, exactly. So call the number on your screen right now and help me—us.

Jason wrung his hands and grinned. Off camera, phone volunteers could be heard apologizing. The image then cut to a still of an ABS mug and a title that said "Technical Difficulties: Please Stand By."

In the concrete cool of the dressing room, Suzanne sighed. She couldn't have asked for a more disastrous opening night. But instead of feeling victorious, a grim fatigue sank in. Nothing could sate her mind. Jason looked like an ass and sounded like an ass. But in this joyless plant of a television station and in this bunker of a dressing room, she didn't care any more. Exhausted and numb, holding a blood-soaked shirt to her face, she licked a trickle of blood from her lip anticipating salt, but tasted nothing.

Angry shouts came from the corridor. She looked at the monitor and saw the opening credits for *Inspector Callaghan*. The prime time break had finished. She heard Jason threatening someone.

"Pull the plug on this now! I'm not going back out there tonight! No way! John's on his way down here, Frank! He'll kick your redneck ass. You're all two-bit nobodies. Fucking Edmonton! Fucking Alberta!"

The dressing room door swung open and Jason slammed it shut. He kicked a gym bag on the floor. Suzanne stirred from the couch and pulled herself up. He kicked over a chair and hurled a hairbrush at the television monitor.

"Something wrong?"

He whipped his head around and noticed Suzanne on the couch, holding one of his shirts to her face.

"What . . . what are you doing with my shirt?! That's fucking expensive!"

She pulled the bloodstained shirt away from her face. Blood trickled into her mouth. She wiped it away with her wrist and eased up off the couch.

Jason made fists and came at her. He breathed in her face, inches away. "Get out. Now. Take your blood and yourself and leave. You freak. I'm telling John all about L.A. I helped you, you know. You don't remember, do you? You were sprawled out in the corridor. I had to look in your pockets for your key and get you in your room. You staggered inside and I had to steer you toward the bed. You just flopped onto it, rolled right over and hit your head on the bedside table. That's how you got your black eye, you disgusting drunk. You're gonna be fired."

Suzanne shook. She stared hard into his narrow eyes. "You fucking moron. You piece of white-trash shit."

He clenched his jaw. "Me? Right back atcha', sister."

She pointed at him. "You did it, didn't you? Let Audi feel you up for money. You were in the pictures with Diana. It was you."

"What pictures? What the hell are you talking about!" Jason's eyes widened. "You're insane. Get out. Get out!"

Suzanne looked down at her shoes and sucked in air. "You can't hide from me any more." She turned away from him and inched toward the door. She open it, took a few steps and fainted.

Epilogue

One Year Later

Alice Foley Dwyer, five and a half months old, sat quietly on Suzanne's lap. Suzanne gripped the baby's sides and gently bounced the infant on her knees. She had to resist the temptation to squeeze the baby too tightly.

"Why do I want to squish her?"

"It's natural," said Jackie, "just don't do it."

Suzanne manoeuvred the baby around awkwardly to face her. Alice wobbled a little and drooled on her yellow jumper.

"Look, she's drooling. Just like her mom used to at last call at Foufounes Électriques."

Suzanne nuzzled the baby's golden head. She grazed the downy surface with her front teeth. The temptation to clamp down and take a bite out of Alice's head made her mouth water.

"Here," she said, handing Jackie the baby, "you'd better take her."

Suzanne stood and went over to the window that faced onto Sherbrooke Street and the fruit stands, video stores, bagel shops and old boutiques below. The sky, blank and empty and as white as the gentle flurries that drifted, diffused the light.

"Do I look okay?" asked Suzanne.

"Do you look okay?" Jackie said. "How do you feel?"

"I . . . don't know."

Suzanne stared at the Resto Café Oxford sign on the corner. A Canada Dry sign used to hang outside the neighbourhood landmark, but she noticed it had been replaced.

"How long has the Canada Dry sign been gone?"

"Years. You're just noticing?"

"Yeah. Things are popping out at me now."

Suzanne was encountering colours and tastes and smells for what seemed liked the first time. Reality had a terrain all its own and she was exploring it, cutting away overgrowth to clear a path. Sober for ten months, still weak and feeble, Suzanne knew that if she went on one more bender she could hemorrhage out. She would have to find pleasure in quieter satisfactions, like knowing that Lawrence hosted the ABS membership pledge breaks once again, that Jason had fled back to Toronto to host an Internet poker site, and that Frank had remained on at ABS after grieving his dismissal with the union. John Brady, word had it, created his own global think tank and moved to an unspecified locale.

"I guess I should get going," said Suzanne, turning to Jackie. "I don't know what I'm going to say."

Jackie cuddled Alice. "Relax."

"I haven't see her in almost thirty-five years."

"So you'll have lots to talk about. Start with the Habs and go from there. Diana's changed from when we were kids. Talk about your new job."

Suzanne zipped up her coat. Diana wanted to reconnect with Suzanne, and Jackie had helped arrange the get-together. Now all Suzanne had to do was show up. She picked at a hangnail. She could talk about her new job as an assistant at the Edmonton library, processing returns and re-stacking shelves. It didn't tax her energy or attention and was the perfect job for someone in early recovery, said her addictions counsellor. Gordon had introduced her to the counsellor at the treatment facility, a place where he had once been an outpatient. He still called Suzanne, even took her to AA meetings. But he wasn't in love with her. Not yet. She held out hope.

"I'm going to put Alice down for a bit," said Jackie.

"I wanna see."

Suzanne followed her into the bedroom, where Jackie nestled the baby in a rocking crib. Alice curled her fingers, cooed and let her head fall to the side. Jackie and Suzanne admired the dozing infant.

"To think we were all that small once," said Suzanne.

"I know."

Suzanne hoped for regeneration, for an exfoliation of her soul. Something was smoothing down her delusions and pet vanities. Was it trust? Wilma would be picking her up at the airport tomorrow in a truck she'd bought herself after completing chemo. Suzanne had promised to bring back bagels. She would keep that promise.

She clasped her hands behind her back and gazed at Alice.

"Jackie, why are you still my friend?"

Jackie brushed her auburn hair away from her face and smiled at Alice. "Because I can't imagine it any other way. Stop stalling. Go see Diana."

"Ten more seconds."

Jackie rocked the crib gently with her foot while Suzanne, her convalescence beginning, gazed at the baby in awe. She couldn't switch it off.

"Seven seconds. Six. Five. Four . . ."

ACKNOWLEDGEMENTS

Thank you to mentors Howard Norman, Richard Scrimger and Antanas Sileika at the Humber School for Writers for your notes, guidance and encouragement. I'll also throw in patience and tolerance.

Thank you to Sarah B. Hood, Kathleen Vaughan, Marion Robb-Gardner, Sarah Cooper, Ken Kidd and Darren Van Dyk for reading earlier drafts of this novel and for your generous feedback. I owe you dinner.

Thank you to Catherine Marjoribanks for the final sweep of the ms and for having a sense of humour.

Shout out to Chris Needham and the staff at NON. Thanks for the breathing room.

Thank you for reading this story.